Anonymous

Life of Thomas Hawley Canfield

His early efforts to open a route for the transportation of the products of

the West to New England

Anonymous

Life of Thomas Hawley Canfield
His early efforts to open a route for the transportation of the products of the West to New England

ISBN/EAN: 9783744727136

Printed in Europe, USA, Canada, Australia, Japan

Cover: Foto ©Raphael Reischuk / pixelio.de

More available books at **www.hansebooks.com**

LIFE OF

THOMAS HAWLEY CANFIELD

HIS EARLY EFFORTS TO OPEN A ROUTE FOR THE TRANSPORTATION
OF THE PRODUCTS OF THE WEST TO NEW ENGLAND,
BY WAY OF THE GREAT LAKES

ST. LAWRENCE RIVER AND VERMONT RAILROADS,

AND

HIS CONNECTION WITH THE EARLY HISTORY OF THE

NORTHERN PACIFIC RAILROAD,

FROM THE

HISTORY OF THE RED RIVER VALLEY, NORTH DAKOTA

AND

PARK REGION OF NORTHWESTERN MINNESOTA.

———

WITH PLATE.

———

BURLINGTON, VERMONT.
1889.

· LIFE OF ·

THOMAS HAWLEY CANFIELD

O MAN is more worthy of an extended and creditable notice in a volume devoted to the eminent men of northern Minnesota than Thomas H. Canfield, who will form the subject of our present article. He is a resident of Lake Park, Minnesota, although on account of extensive interests in Burlington, Vermont, much of his time is spent in the East. A history of his life is, to a great extent, a history of the inception and inauguration of that great enterprise, the Northern Pacific Railroad, as he was one of the founders, and to him, more than to any other one man, was due its organization and getting it into some practical form and system in its early days. He has, therefore, been closely identified with the growth and development of the Northwest, and his name is indissolubly associated with the history of both State and Nation. A man of broad ideas, wonderful vitality and energy, unconquerable will and indefatigable perseverance, the history of the gigantic enterprises which he has inaugurated and placed in shape for successful consummation, demonstrate the characteristics of the man. A man of the strictest integrity, kind and courteous, of extensive reading and observation, together with his keen foresight and executive abilities, he has indelibly impressed his individuality upon the history of the great undertakings with which he has been connected. The generation in which we live has scarcely furnished a more worthy subject for the pen of the biographer.

GENEALOGY.

James De Philo, a French Huguenot and citizen of Normandy, France, in the sixteenth century, in reward for meritorious services to the crown of England, received honorable mention, a new cognomen and a grant of land on the river "Cam," county of Yorkshire, England, to which he removed and afterward occupied as a loyal subject of the crown. He received the cognomen of "Cam," in distinction of the land grant. Subsequently from "Cam De Philo" the name was changed in England in the sixteenth century to "Cam-philo," then to

"Camphilo," and by his descendants in 1639, in New Haven, Connecticut, to "Camphield." Later in Milford, Connecticut, in 1680, to "Camfield," and still later in Milford, in 1720, to "Canfield," which has since been retained by the descendants in the United States.

One of his descendants, Thomas Canfield, and Phebe Crane, his wife, came to Milford, Connecticut, in 1646, and he died there August 22, 1689. His son Jeremiah, who was born in 1660, resided in Milford until 1727, when he removed to New Milford and died in 1739. He had ten children. The ninth son, Zerubbabel, in 1733 married Mary Bostwick, and they became the parents of eight children. Their third child, Nathan, was born July 28, 1739, in New Milford, Connecticut, and removed to Arlington, Bennington county, Vermont, in 1768. For his first wife he married, November 14, 1765, Lois Hard, a daughter of James Hard, by whom he had four children. After her death he married Betsy Burton, by whom he had seven sons and one daughter. Samuel, the sixth son, was born in Arlington, January 2, 1792, and died September 28, 1840. He was the father of the subject of this sketch.

Now to trace the genealogy on the mother's side: Joseph Hawley, who was born in Derbyshire, England, in 1603, came to Stratford, Connecticut, and died in 1690. He had eight children, five sons and three daughters. His oldest child, Samuel, was born in Stratford, Connecticut, in 1647, and married for his first wife, May 20, 1673, Mary Thompson, grand-daughter of Governor Welles of Farmington, Connecticut. They had six sons and one daughter. After her death he married a second time, and had four sons and one daughter. He died August 24, 1734. Ephraim, the oldest child by the second marriage, was born in New Milford, Connecticut, in 1690, and married, October 5, 1711,

Sarah Curtiss, of Stratford, Connecticut, and removed to Arlington, Vermont, where he died in 1771, and was buried in the churchyard adjoining the church. They had eight sons and two daughters. Their oldest child, Jehiel, was born in New Milford, Connecticut, February 14, 1712, and married Sarah Dunning, March 30, 1731, and removed to Arlington, Vermont, about 1764. They had five sons and five daughters. Andrew, their oldest child, was born June 22, 1732, at Newtown, now Bridgeport, Connecticut, and married, January 2, 1757, Ann, a daughter of James Hard. He died June 24, 1801. They had ten children—seven sons and three daughters. Eli, their oldest child, was born in New Milford, Connecticut, November 20, 1757; removed to Arlington, Vermont, and married, November 4, 1787, Mary Jeffers, of Chaleur, Lower Canada, and died at Alton, Illinois, January 19, 1850. They had four sons and one daughter, Mary Ann, who was born November 6, 1795, in New Carlisle, on bay of Chaleur, Province of Lower Canada, and was married to Samuel Canfield, in Arlington, by the Rev. Abraham Bronson, October 29, 1820, and died July 22, 1825. They had two children, one a daughter, Marion, born January 2, 1824, in Arlington, and married to the Rev. Fletcher J. Hawley, D. D., by the Right Rev. Bishop Hopkins, in St. Paul's Church, Burlington, Vermont, November 2, 1853, and now residing at Lake Park, Minnesota; the other a son, Thomas Hawley Canfield, the subject of this sketch, who was born at Arlington, Bennington county, Vermont, March 29, 1822.

Vermont, especially that part west of the Green mountains, was mostly settled by people from Connecticut, commencing about 1760, who received the titles to their lands by charter from Benning Wentworth, the colonial governor of New Hampshire. Several families had come to Arlington to make it their home, among them the Can-fields, Hawleys, Hards, Allens and Bakers, the most prominent. The new settlers went on to improve their lands and fix up their new homes, when they were startled, July 20, 1764, by a decision of the crown that the territory was adjudged to be under the jurisdiction of New York, supposing that the great seal of a royal governor was a sufficient guarantee that their titles were valid. Hence there arose at once the great question of the conflicting claims of New York and New Hampshire, over the territory known as Vermont, in which each State attempted either to control the whole or at least to divide the territory between them, and thus obliterate Vermont completely as a separate Territory and from ever becoming an independent State in the future. This involved a long and bitter controversy between New Hampshire and New York, which, together with the increasing feeling among the colonies of hostility to England, placed the settlers in a very unpleasant, not to say dangerous, situation. Bordering, as Vermont did, upon Canada, subject upon the slightest provocation to attacks from the British, and with Lake Champlain upon her western border, which was the great route of the English between New York and Montreal, her territory became the battleground between the three contending parties, with England upon the one hand endeavoring to prevent her from joining the other colonies in their movement for independence, while New York and New Hampshire desired to blot her out entirely. Under such circumstances the situation of a mere handful of settlers was very trying as well as dangerous, and required not only great bravery, patriotism and courage but great wisdom, forethought and prudent action in the management of their affairs, bringing to the front men of the most varied ability and different views. Some turbulent spirits like Gen. Ethan Allen, Remember Baker and

Col. Seth Warner were ready to declare open hostility against all the claimants, while others like Chittenden, Hawley and Canfield, of a more mild, conservative and prudent character, were disposed to move more cautiously, awaiting the development of events. Arlington was the great central point of all operations. Here was the headquarters of the "Council of Safety," which had unlimited powers for government of the State; here resided Thomas Chittenden, its president, the George Washington of Vermont, who was afterward elected governor of the State for twenty years. Here lived Gen. Ethan Allen, the hero of Ticonderoga, who, with a handful of Green Mountain boys, demanded its surrender in the name of the "Great Jehovah and the Continental Congress." Here assembled his companions and associates, Remember Baker, Col. Seth Warner and others, to concoct their plans to resist the New Yorkers and to teach them that the "gods of the valleys were not the gods of the hills."

Capt. Jehiel Hawley and Nathan Canfield, from their well-known sound judgment and common sense, as well as irreproachable private characters and high moral worth, became the leaders, and for some time managed and controlled this chaotic people. After all other attempts had failed to satisfy New York of the justice of the title to their possessions from New Hampshire, at a meeting held October 21, 1772, Capt. Jehiel Hawley and James Breckenridge were sent to England to lay before King George III. the state of affairs, and succeeded in getting an order from the king forbidding the governor of New York from interfering with the titles and lands granted by the governor of New Hampshire. With this decision of the crown in their favor, Hawley and Breckenridge returned, expecting that it would settle all disputes, and the settlers naturally expected to go on in peace and clear up the wilderness. But the order of the king was but little regarded by the general assembly of New York, which offered a bounty of £50 for the apprehension of either of the leaders. Up to this time the people of this section were substantially one, a common danger compelling all to unite. But this act of the general assembly of New York aroused to action all classes, and was answered by a series of resolutions of a general meeting " of the committees of the several townships on the west side of the Green mountains," held at the house of Jehiel Hawley on the third Wednesday of March, 1774, counseling resistance to all encroachments of New York. To show how determined these people were to maintain their rights against great superiority of numbers, in 1774 Dr. Samuel Adams, holding lands under title from New Hampshire, exasperated his neighbors by advising them to re-purchase their lands from New York. He was arrested and carried to the Green Mountain Tavern at Bennington, where the committee heard his defense and then ordered him to be tied to an arm chair and hoisted up to the sign (a catamount skin, stuffed, sitting upon the sign-post, twenty-five feet from the ground, with large teeth grinning toward New York), and there hung two hours in sight of the people, as a punishment merited by his enmity to the rights and liberties of the people. January 26, 1775, Benjamin Hough, of Clarendon, a Baptist minister who had just obtained a commission from New York as justice of the peace, was arrested by General Ethan Allen and tied to an apple tree in front of his house at Sunderland and whipped, in pursuance of a sentence of the committee of safety. In England Capt. Jehiel Hawley was treated with the most flattering marks of respect, by several of the prominent men, and especially by the Earl of Dartmouth ; such was the estimation in which his prudence and judgment was held by the co-

partners in the agency, that they would never act as a board without his presence, and by his means chiefly the Vermont claims were substantiated.

During all this time from 1764, amid all the accessions to this colony from Connecticut and elsewhere, there was no minister of any denomination. Captain Jehiel Hawley was the acknowledged leader, to whom all, even the most turbulent spirits, yielded. He built the first frame house in Arlington, and, being a man of high moral character and a devoted and exemplary communicant of the Church of England, to his house, Sunday after Sunday, the people from all parts of the surrounding country came for public worship. Captain Hawley read the service of the Church of England and a sermon, the "Protestant Episcopal Church in the United States" at this early day not having been regularly organized in America. The difficulties of the times delayed the building of a church, although the services were kept up regularly by Captain Hawley, which formed the nucleus of a congregation, and in 1784 a parish was organized. Two shillings on a pound were levied on the inhabitants to build the church, now St. James church, Arlington—the original building having been replaced by a stone one on the same site in 1832 — which was the first Episcopal church organized in Vermont. In 1787 this parish was represented in the convention of the Protestant Episcopal Church, at Stratford, Connecticut, by Nathan Canfield, the first delegate.

Notwithstanding the continued aggressions of New York the inhabitants, under the leadership of Captain Hawley, were making rapid improvements, when a new trouble was approaching in 1775. The trouble between the colonies and England had culminated and the battle of Lexington opened the War of the Revolution. A convention of the people of Vermont was called in

1776 to draft a constitution, which was done, declaring Vermont an independent State; but before the constitution could be ratified by the people General Burgoyne, with his splendid army of 10,000 men, had entered Lake Champlain and anchored in Vermont waters. It became necessary, to meet the emergency, to form a provisional government without an hour's delay, and a "Council of Safety" was appointed, invested with all the powers of government, both civil and military. Its power was unlimited and absolute, and, in fact, the urgency was so great that it was necessary to place in the hands of the fourteen men composing the "Council of Safety" the legislative, executive and judicial powers of the State, and intrust them with the life, liberty and property of every individual. It was a dark hour—no money in the treasury, no time for taxation, no credit to borrow; desperate measures were necessary. A commission of sequestration was appointed, "invested with full authority to seize the goods and chattels of all persons who had or should join the common enemy, sell them at public vendue and the proceeds to be paid over to the treasurer to be appointed by the council."

The council of safety as well as commissioners of sequestration made their headquarters at Arlington. Thomas Chittenden, afterward governor of the State for twenty years, was its president, and Ira Allen, brother of Gen. Ethan Allen, its secretary. This sudden change of affairs compelled the people at once to decide what course to pursue, whether to join the revolutionists or remain loyal to the crown, whence they had received by gift all their lands and possessions. It was a very trying time, especially with the commissioners of sequestration encamped among them, urged on by such tumultuous spirits as Ethan Allen, Seth Warner and Remember Baker, to seize, upon the slightest shadow of loyalty

to England, the property of any one and confiscate it. The town was in a critical position. Most of its inhabitants, while feeling grateful for all that had been done for them by the crown, felt that it would be better for the colonies to be an independent nation; but whether the time had come to throw off the yoke of the mother country was the question; and whether, if overthrowing a good government then existing, they would be assured that the Revolution would succeed and a better one arise out of the wreck, or whether anarchy and chaos would be the result for a long time to come. It was a difficult question to determine, especially after having been several years in conflict with New York, and now, by the order of King George III., sustained in the position they had taken.

If the powers of the existing government were shaken off, where was the power of re-organization? "Committees of Safety" had been accepted as a necessity, and if the laws then existing were overthrown, the prospect was, they would be subject to the powers of these committees for an indefinite length of time. Is it strange that men with property and families should hesitate? There were uneasy spirits among the inhabitants as in all communities, who disliked labor and, expecting to live by there wits, were ready for any change by which something might turn up to their advantage. There were others who took a more comprehensive view, and were ready to risk everything from truly patriotic motives for the great principles of political freedom. Unfortunately these were not the men of property and influence. The leading men of the new State were very indignant, especially as the British army of 10,000 men under General Burgoyne was on its way from Canada. Public excitement became very great, especially as there were no railroads or telegraphs in those days to keep the people informed of the rapidity of his approach. Names of men from all parts of the State were mentioned who were suspected of Toryism. The Council of Safety met frequently at Arlington, and woe be to the tory who was suspected of loyalty to the crown. It was a trying time—there was no time for delay. Families were divided among themselves; neighbors arrayed against each other, some joined the revolutionists, others remained loyal to the king and left for Canada, while others, "who did not think it right to rebel against a king who had done them no harm," remained at their homes, submitting to the powers of the government *de facto*, believing that colonies so far from the mother country ought at some time to be independent, but was this the time? This was sufficient cause in the eyes of the commissioners of sequestration, backed up by restless spirits, to seize their property and confiscate it. Captain Jehiel Hawley may be said to have belonged to this last class. His high moral worth, peaceful manners and kind consideration and friendship for all the settlers for so many years long secured him from molestation. His age was such that there was little danger of his going to the enemy and he could not well be a fighting man. But the extensive property which he and his family possessed was a strong temptation to the sequestrators. Anonymous letters were sent to him threatening midnight assassination, and there were circumstances that satisfied him that the writers would not shrink from making their words good. Yielding to an emergency, which he regarded necessary to save his life, he abandoned his entire worldly wealth and started for Canada, and died on his way on Lake Champlain, November 2, 1777, and was buried at "Quaker Smith's" point on the shores of the lake in Shelburne, Vermont. It was a sad day to Arlington when Jehiel Hawley left the settlement, mainly of his own planting, to seek safety in Canada. Thus ended the life of this truly great and good man, of whom it may be said his enemies could find no fault. The late Chief Justice of Vermont, Hon. Charles K. Williams, said to Samuel Canfield, "that undoubtedly Capt. Jehiel Hawley was the ablest man in his day in Vermont."

Nathan Canfield remained at Arlington during the war. He was the leading business spirit of the town, merchant, landlord, justice of the peace and town representative after Vermont became a State. He built a large saw mill and furnace for smelting iron ore, the first in the State, organized the first church, and at his house the preliminary arrangements for the first convention of the Protestant Episcopal Church in Vermont were made 100 years ago. The house he built is still standing, and in it Samuel Canfield and his son, Thomas Hawley Canfield, were born.

At this distant day it is very difficult to understand the difficulties and dangers of those troublesome times, and the fact that two such men as Jehiel Hawley and Nathan Canfield could have passed through them all, retaining the confidence of the whole community, managing the public business to the satisfaction of all factions, demonstrates that they were men of uncommon judgment and common sense, as well as extraordinary character for integrity and ability.

Samuel Canfield inherited many of the prominent traits of his father, Nathan Canfield, and from 1820 to 1840, the time of his death, was the leading man of Arlington, and during the most of that time was sheriff or deputy sheriff of the county of Bennington, an office of prominence and distinction in those days. He became one of the most popular men in that portion of the State, practically controlling the politics of the county. He was a man of fine stature, cheerful and persuasive manners, a good judge of men, upright, reliable, energetic, the soul of honor, and true as steel to his friends. He died September 29, 1840, being at that time representative-elect to the legislature of Vermont from Arlington. His wife, Mary Ann Hawley, great-granddaughter of Capt. Jehiel Hawley, above mentioned, possessed many of the traits of her ancestors. A lady of commanding presence, attractive features, charming manners and bright intellect, of rare executive ability, universally respected and the acknowledged leader in every society where she was known. She died July 22, 1825, leaving her only son, at three years of age, Thomas Hawley Canfield.

Such were his ancestors and such the trying times in which they lived.

THOMAS HAWLEY CANFIELD,

whose name heads our present article, was brought up on a farm, rising early and working from morning to night with the men, taking his share in every kind of work until he became familiar with all the details of farm work, which, with the habits of order, economy and management then formed, have been of great service to him in after years. His early education was obtained mostly in the common schools of his native town, although he soon evinced a strong desire for something more advanced than they afforded. Accordingly, he was placed by his father at Burr Seminary, in Manchester, Vermont, at its opening in May, 1833, under those able professors, the Rev. Dr. Lyman Coleman, the Rev. Dr. John H. Worcester, John Aiken, Esq., and Wm. A. Burnham, where he remained until he was fitted for college at the age of fourteen. Notwithstanding the standard of this seminary was very high, and he the youngest pupil among 150, all much older than himself, yet he acquitted himself very creditably, taking the highest rank in all his classes.

Having a decided taste for practical matters, and not desiring to enter college at this early age, he returned home to the work of the farm for two years, when he was transferred to the Troy Episcopal Institute with reference to a scientific course of study, which had a very efficient corps of instructors, among them the present Bishop of Vermont.

He was particularly fond of mathematics, and it was while demonstrating a difficult problem at a public examination in the city of Troy, New York, that he, although an entire stranger, arrested the attention of the late Bishop Alonzo Potter, of Pennsylvania, who was one of the examiners, and then the acting president of Union College, Schenectady, New York. The principal of the Troy Episcopal Institute subsequently published an arithmetic for schools, based mostly upon problems and examples which he had prepared and which were worked out and solved for him by young Canfield. President Potter became so interested in the promptness and accuracy with which he disposed of all examples presented to him that he determined to insist upon the young man having a higher and broader education, and finally prevailed upon him to abandon his idea of becoming a civil engineer and to enter the junior class in Union College in the fall of 1839. It was a very trying ordeal for him to pass through, being by far the youngest in a class of over eighty, who had had all the advantages of the freshman and sophomore years, but yet, through the same indefatigable energy and perseverance which had characterized his conduct thus far in life in everything which he had undertaken, he was one of the "*maximum ten*" who came out at the head of the class. Soon after the beginning of the senior year he was summoned to Vermont by the sudden death of his father, and although strongly urged by President Potter, who, during the junior year, had taken great interest in him and offered

to assist him to any position he should want
after graduation, as well as by his own rel-
atives, to return and complete his college
course, he considered the duty he owed to
his mother and only sister paramount to
everything else, and again took up the burden of the farm, and thus, at the early age
of eighteen, his business life began, which
has continued constant· and uninterrupted
to the present day.

In addition to the cares and duties of the
farm, he was active in all public matters
having for their object the improvement and
well-being of society. He organized a
lyceum, established debating societies, and
procured prominent lecturers upon various
subjects (among them Colonel Crockett),
which, during the winter months, called out
crowded houses. About this time a new
element appeared in the temperance movement, the coming out on the stage of "six
reformed drunkards from Baltimore," who
took the platform throughout the country,
and were enabled by their own experience
to portray more vividly than had ever been
done before the terrible consequences which
followed in the trail of intemperance. Mr.
Canfield organized a series of meetings in
Arlington and adjoining towns, and secured
one of these men to address them as well as
himself, and soon had enrolled upon the
total abstinence pledge large numbers, the
result of which was a great improvement in
the morals of the community.

Finding the labor of the farm too severe
for his slender constitution, he removed, in
1844, to Williston, Vermont, where he became
a merchant, having in the meantime married Elizabeth A., only daughter of Eli Chittenden, a grandson of Thomas Chittenden,
the first governor of Vermont. She died in
1848, and he subsequently married Caroline
A., the youngest daughter of the Rt. Rev.
Bishop Hopkins, of Vermont, a charming
and accomplished lady, who is still living,

and by whom he has two sons and three
daughters—Emily, John Henry Hopkins,
Marion, Flora and Thomas H., Jr., all now
engaged in completing their education in
Burlington, Vermont, at the Diocesan Church
Schools and the University of Vermont.

REMOVAL TO BURLINGTON.

In addition to the ordinary business of
merchandise, Mr. Canfield added to it the purchase of the products of the country, butter,
cheese, wool, starch, cattle, sheep, horses and
everything which the farm raised, thereby
carrying out the idea of home protection
and creating a home market for their produce. Here he built up and carried on an
extensive business under very pleasant circumstances until April, 1847, when he
removed to Burlington, Vermont, where he
still resides, to take the place in the firm of
Follett & Bradley, the leading wholesale
merchants and forwarders in northern Vermont, made vacant by the withdrawal of
Judge Follett, who had taken the presidency
of the Rutland & Burlington Railroad,
then in course of construction. Mr. Canfield
for some time resisted this arrangement,
believing himself too young and inexperienced for the important position tendered
him, but finally was induced to yield to the
persistent entreaties of Follett & Bradley,
who had recognized in his short business
career at Williston the peculiar traits in his
character which fitted him particularly for the
responsible position which they desired him
to occupy. Their office and headquarters were
at the stone store on Water street, Burlington, near the steamer wharf and railroad
depot. As there were no railroads in
Vermont in those days, all of the produce of every kind of the farm, mine or
manufactory came to Burlington for shipment to market, and the goods for the merchants in the country, from Boston and
New York, came here in return. To accom-

modate and facilitate this business, Bradley & Canfield had extensive wharves and warehouses, as well as a line of boats to New York and Boston for the transportation of this property both ways, their wharves also being the regular landing place of the passenger steamers and other vessels, resulting in an extensive business, requiring not only much capital, but also great care and ability to manage this part of it, which devolved principally upon Mr. Canfield. About this time, Professor Morse having brought his telegraph into practical operation between the principal cities, Mr. Canfield, in connection with Professor Benedict, the Hon. Ezra Cornell, founder of Cornell University, and Colonel John H. Peck, got up a line between Montreal and Troy, New York. Mr. Canfield visited Vergennes, Orwell, Middlebury, Rutland and many other towns along the line, getting stockholders and organizing the company; and on the 2d day of February, 1848, the first message passed:

From the City of Troy to the City of Burlington:

We do sincerely congratulate you as having become, at this early day, one of those favored communities, united by the life blood of speedy communication, and as sincerely congratulate ourselves on being able to salute, face to face the queen city of Lake Champlain.

FIRST RAILROAD IN VERMONT.

But the time had come for Vermont to be invaded by railroads from Boston; one via Concord and Montpelier, and the other via Fitchburg, Bellows Falls and Rutland, were being extended across the Green mountains by two different routes to Burlington. His firm, Bradley & Canfield, with two or three other gentlemen, were engaged in building the one from Bellows Falls by the way of Rutland, which was completed in December, 1849. At the same time, in connection with George W. Strong, of Rutland, and Merritt Clark, of Poultney, they built the Rutland & Washington Railroad from Rutland to Eagle Bridge, New York, connecting at that point with a railroad to Troy and another to Albany, thus opening the first line of railroad to New York as well as to Boston from northwestern Vermont. While these were in progress Messrs. Bradley & Canfield, in connection with T. F. Strong and Joseph and Selah Chamberlin, built the Ogdensburgh Railroad from Rouse's Point to Ogdensburgh, as well as other railroads in New York and Pennsylvania. Mr. Canfield was now fairly enlisted with a fleet of boats in the transportation business between Montreal, Vermont and New York, as well as in mercantile pursuits and in the building of railroads, which at that time but few contractors undertook. In the management of these great interests Mr. Canfield formed an extensive acquaintance and gained a knowledge of the resources of the country on both sides of Lake Champlain, which gave him an experience in handling and transporting the products of the country that attracted the attention of the directors of the Rutland & Washington Railroad, and commended him as a fit man to manage its affairs, and to open and organize it for business. As soon as completed they selected him for superintendent, which he declined. But so many of his friends were interested in it, and it being a new departure in the transportation of western Vermont, he yielded to their appeals and accepted the situation, retaining at the same time the management of his former business at Burlington. Mr. Canfield afterward became president of the Rutland & Washington Railroad, and subsequently took a lease of it and operated it on his own account, being probably the first railroad in the country ever leased by a private individual. It was while Mr. Canfield had this lease that Jay Gould appeared upon the stage, and endeavored at an annual meeting of the stockholders by a *coup d'etat* to get control of the road, but he found his match in Mr. Canfield, who had anticipated his plans and completely defeated them. Subsequently, after the termination of the lease and surrender by Mr. Canfield of the road to the trustees, Mr. Gould acquired an interest, and afterward controlled, which laid the foundation of his subsequent notable and prosperous career.

The operating of railroads was then comparatively in its infancy, and there were few experienced men to be employed. He at once instituted a rigid system of discipline and accountability, in which at first he met with opposition; but after a time all became impressed with the justice and importance of it, and he received the hearty co operation of the employés and directors, and thus established an *esprit de corps* among all connected with it which made the "Eagle Bridge Route" celebrated for its promptness, speed and regularity, its accomodation to the traveling and business public, and its employés as among the best railroad men in the country.

Heretofore it required two days for the mails as well as passengers to go between Burlington or Montreal and New York. Mr. Canfield first proposed to make a day line between the cities. He went to New York to enlist Governor Morgan, then president of the Hudson River Railroad, in the plan, but he was coldly received by him, for the reason that the governor believed it was simply impossible. But after several interviews the governor consented to make the trial for three months, on condition that Mr. Canfield would guarantee his company from any loss. It is 300 miles from New York to Burlington, and about four hundred to Montreal, which involved an average speed of about forty miles an hour. Accordingly, on the 15th day of May, 1852, at 6 o'clock A. M., a train left the Chambers' street depot in New York, Mr. French, super-

intendent of the Hudson River Railroad, Mr. Johnson, superintendent of the Troy & Boston Railroad, and Mr. Canfield with two or three reporters, being all that would risk their lives upon such a crazy experiment. The train arrived at Rutland on time at 1:25 P. M., having made the run from Eagle Bridge, sixty-two miles, in eighty-five minutes, making five stops, with Nat. Gooken, engineer, and Amos Story, conductor. Burlington was reached at 3:20 P. M., and Montreal at 7 P. M. But for the fact that it had on board the New York papers of that morning it would have been impossible to have made the public believe that it came from beyond Troy. Thus was settled a question of great importance, the establishing of a daily intercourse between Montreal and New York, since which time two daily trains have been kept up most of the time.

Burlington, previous to the advent of railroads, had been the commercial center of northern Vermont, and had been built up from the trade arising from its being the point of shipment to the New York and Boston markets of the produce of the country, and the receipt and distribution of merchandise in return. Large numbers of eight and ten-horse teams from Woodstock, Northfield, Bradford, St. Johnsbury, Hyde Park, Derby Line, Montpelier and other places, with their loads of starch, butter, cheese, wool, scales and manufactured goods, kept up a lively business with the interior, bringing to Burlington much money to be exchanged for flour, salt, iron, steel, nails and other merchandise. In addition to this the lines of boats running to Troy, Albany, New York, Montreal, and all points on the lake, created an active and prosperous business for Burlington, and it became a very thriving and beautiful town.

When the question came up of connecting by railroad Boston and Burlington, two routes were proposed, one via Montpelier and Concord, and the other via Rutland and Fitchburg. There was much difference of opinion among the citizens which would be most for the interest of Burlington, or in other words, which would injure it the least, or least interfere with its already prosperous business. Public meetings were held, much excitement and feeling prevailed; one party, headed by the old established house of J. & J. H. Peck & Co., advocating the Vermont Central route via Montpelier, of which Governor Charles Paine became president, and the other party, represented by Bradley & Canfield, urging the Rutland line, of which Judge Follett became president, who maintained that as Burlington had always derived its business more or less from eastern and northeastern Vermont, and parts of New Hampshire adjacent, that a railroad from Boston, penetrating these sections, would divert the trade direct to Boston, and thereby injure Burlington correspondingly; while from the south Burlington had never had any trade, the connection with market from that portion of Vermont being made directly with the different shipping ports on the lake, and hence it was evident that while Burlington had nothing to lose, but every thing to gain by opening a trade with the towns of western and southern Vermont, at the same time the line to Boston would be shorter than by Montpelier, and, besides, a connection could be made at Rutland with railroads to Troy and Albany, and thus have a direct rail communication with New York and the West in the winter as well as in the summer. The result of this controversy was the building of both lines, which was greatly accelerated by the powerful aid and influence contributed by the two contending parties, and on the 18th of December, 1849, the first train from Boston via Rutland came into Burlington, and on the 25th day of the same month the first train via Montpelier arrrived at Winooski, the bridge over the

river at that place not being finished to admit it to Burlington. With the advent of the Vermont Central train the fine ten-horse teams of Governor Paine and others ceased their trips forever to Burlington, and the elegant and celebrated six-horse teams and coaches of Cottrell and Shattuck, of Montpelier, took their departure for the last time, as had before much of the business from that part of the State; and the prostration and decline of Burlington began, and stagnation in business reigned supreme, as Bradley & Canfield had maintained would be the case if the Vermont Central line was built.

Originally, to counteract the injury to a certain extent which might arise to Burlington from a diversion of its business by the Central line, it was contended by its friends that, its terminus being in Burlington with its shops, offices, etc., new business would be created to offset in part the loss of the old. It was also understood that an independent railroad should be built from Burlington north to Canada to accommodate both the Boston lines, which were to make their termini in Burlington. But the excitement ran so high during the building that Governor Paine, after becoming sure that his line would be built, gave up coming to Burlington, and arranged, with the aid of John Smith and Lawrence Brainerd, of St. Albans, and Joseph Clark, of Milton, three of the shrewdest and most capable business men ever raised in Vermont, to make a line north from Essex Junction, thus practically extending the main line of the Central to Rouse's Point, leaving Burlington at one side to be reached by a branch of six miles. This move gave the final blow to Burlington, and left the Rutland Railroad without any rail connection north, and forced it to make its connections with the Ogdensburgh and Champlain and St. Lawrence Railroads to Montreal, at Rouse's Point by boat. To meet this emergency, as the Rutland Railroad Company had not the right by its charter to build boats, Bradley & Canfield came to the rescue, and within ninety days, early in the spring of 1850, constructed four barges of the capacity of 3,000 barrels of flour each, and the steamer "Boston" to tow them between Burlington and Rouse's Point; and this enabled the Rutland line to compete successfully for the western business with the Vermont Central.

FIRST CARGO OF FLOUR BY THE ST. LAWRENCE ROUTE.

Previous to this, as early as 1847, Mr. Canfield felt that a change in the character of the business at Burlington was inevitable so soon as the railroads should be completed, and to supply what would be destroyed new branches would have to be built up. All the flour and salt heretofore, for northern Vermont and New York, came from Troy and Albany by canal via Whitehall, while that for the rest of New England, after passing through the Erie canal, found its way to Boston and other ports either by water, by way of New York, or by the Boston & Albany Railroad to the inland towns. He thus early took the ground that, with the new proposed lines of railroads completed between the Atlantic and River St. Lawrence, a new route would have to be opened by that way and the upper lakes to the wheat regions of the West. Upon consultation with leading forwarders at Troy and Albany, a movement of this kind, he found, would incur the hostility of New York and all parties interested in the navigation of the Erie canal, which at that time was the main channel of transportation between the lakes and Hudson river. But Mr. Canfield, nothing daunted by such intimations, went in the spring of 1848 to Montreal, and laid his views and plans for a northern route before Messrs. Holmes, Young & Knapp, the most prominent merchants in Canada, and who carried

on an extensive business with Cleveland, Detroit and Chicago in wheat, flour and pork. They concurred with him in the desirability, but not the practicability of the scheme. From thence he went up the St. Lawrence river, stopping at Ogdensburgh, Kingston, Sackett's Harbor, Oswego, Rochester and Buffalo, to Cleveland. Here he met Messrs. A. H. & D. N. Barney, who were engaged in boating on the western lakes, and who have since become so prominent in the railroad and express business in New York City, and engaged them to send a vessel with a load of flour to Montreal, which he purchased on his own account. This vessel, although passing the locks in the Welland and St. Lawrence canals to Montreal, was too large to pass those of the Chambly into Lake Champlain, and hence Mr. Canfield had to unload the flour at Montreal, and after much trouble with the custom-house officers transferred it by ferry-boat to La Prairie, nine miles above Montreal, on the opposite side of the St. Lawrence, thence by rail to St. Johns, at the foot of Lake Champlain, and then by steamer to Burlington. This was the first cargo of flour ever sent from Lake Erie to Lake Champlain via Welland canal and St. Lawrence river, and the entering-wedge which Mr. Canfield then believed, and still believes, to a great water communication from the west end of Lake Superior to Lake Champlain, by which steam vessels of much larger size than any now on the lakes, will make the whole passage without breaking bulk, and ultimately going through to New York by the conversion of the Champlain canal between Whitehall and Troy into a ship canal. Although it was an expensive experiment, yet it showed that there was another route than that by the Erie canal, which was sooner or later to be developed into an important one. The next season Bradley & Canfield, in order to more fully demonstrate the practicability of their new route, chartered the steam propeller "Earl of Cathcart" to run between Detroit and Montreal, agreeing to furnish at Detroit 1,500 barrels of flour every two weeks, at a fixed rate of freight, to be paid whether the flour was shipped or not; and to enable them to comply with this contract they purchased a large flouring mill at Battle Creek, Michigan, to manufacture the flour, and stationed Eli Chittenden at Detroit to attend to the shipments, and thus opened a regular trade via Montreal to Burlington the whole season.

FIRST LINE OF PROPELLERS FROM THE UPPER LAKES TO OGDENSBURGH.

Meanwhile the Ogdensburgh Railroad was completed, and Mr. Canfield, still determined to carry out his original plan of opening a more practicable northern route for much of the business between New England and the West, went to Oswego and Buffalo, and after investigating more fully the operations of steam propellers on the lakes and Welland canal, made a contract with E. C. Bancroft, of Oswego, to build two propellers of full size for the Welland canal locks, costing $20,000 each, and arranged with Chamberlin & Crawford, at Cleveland, to supply two more, with which to make a regular line from Detroit to Ogdensburgh. The Erie canal forwarders, becoming alarmed at this new departure, procured from the legislature of New York a reduction of tolls on wheat and flour, which interfered seriously with the new route, compelling a reduction of price of freight to about actual cost. This reduction was unnecessary, as it did not alter the production, and Mr. Canfield contended that the increased production of grain in the new-developed Western States would keep pace with all the increased facilities of transportation, which has since proved to be true, notwithstanding there are now eight through lines of railroad, as well as the Erie canal and various water lines

on the St. Lawrence river. Very few people at that day could be induced to concur in Mr. Canfield's views of the future development of the great Northwest, and in looking back now it is as difficult to realize why they could not. But for the broad views and almost prophetic ideas of a few such men, backed up by tremendous energy and perseverance, the great internal improvements of this country might yet be comparatively in their infancy.

The next season, 1850, opened with the line of propellers between Ogdensburgh and Detroit. But the fates were against them. One of the new ones with a large cargo ran onto a rock in the upper St. Lawrence and sank on the first trip, and another was wrecked on her second voyage, entailing a very heavy loss upon Bradley & Canfield. Others were immediately procured to take their places, and the line was kept up, so that it was demonstrated at the end of the season that with proper vessels a regular line could be supported, the result of which was the establishment of the Northern Transportation Line from Ogdensburgh to Detroit and Chicago, consisting of a fleet of ten or fifteen propellers, which forever settled the practicability of the Northern route, so that at the present day nearly all the business between northern New England and the West is done that way, either by rail or water. During the four or five years of its inauguration Mr. Canfield was the main advocate and promoter of it, and it was through his persistent efforts and repeated journeys between Burlington and the various ports on the St. Lawrence and upper lakes, and after various trials and experiments and great loss of time and money, that he saw his plans succeed and the route thoroughly opened and maintained.

CAUGHNAWAGA SHIP CANAL.

But there were some obstacles which he still encountered and especially the delay and damage incident to transhipment at different points, which led him to consider the plan of a continuous water route without transhipment from the upper lakes, involving the construction of a ship canal from Caughnawaga, above the Lachine Rapids, in the St. Lawrence river, to Lake Champlain. He had frequent interviews in Montreal with the Hon. John Young, Benjamin Holmes, Harrison Stephens, Peter McGill, Messrs. Holton & McPherson, forwarders, all of whom were men of broad views and extended knowledge of the resources of the vast West on both sides of the line. Mr. Young had already agitated the subject in Canada, and there was no man in the States or Dominion who was better informed upon the subject, or who could present it in a more convincing and magnetic manner. Mr. Canfield arranged a series of meetings to bring the scheme before the public. One was held in Burlington, August 14, 1849, which was addressed by Mr. Young, Judge Follett and Charles Adams, Esq., of Burlington, the latter gentleman entering into it very enthusiastically as well as intelligently. Another was held at Saratoga, August 21, over which General John E. Wool presided, which was also addressed by Mr. Young, Mr. Adams, Chancellor Walworth and many other prominent men from Montreal, Troy, Albany, Whitehall and other cities. A committee was appointed, consisting of prominent citizens in the States and Canada, to devise measures to carry on the enterprise. A survey was made, and it looked as though the project might be accomplished. But when the matter came up in the Parliament of Canada for a charter an unexpected resistance arose from Montreal, and although the charter was finally granted, there were so many impracticable conditions attached to it, that Mr. Young and his friends did not deem it wise to proceed under its provisions.

The fact that the large lumber trade with Canada and Michigan has grown up since at Burlington, even with the much inferior and more distant connection by the way of the Chambly Canal, demonstrates the necessity of a canal of much larger dimensions, and had the original plan of Mr. Canfield and Mr. Young been carried out, Burlington would long since have become the distributing point for the flour and grain of the West as well as lumber for nearly all of New England ; the large steamers leaving Duluth and Chicago would have discharged their cargoes on the docks at Burlington without breaking bulk, thereby creating a business which would have added greatly to its population and prosperity, and made it one of the most important cities of New England. Mr. Canfield still believes that this canal will, sooner or later, be built ; that the necessities of trade and commerce will demand it, and that nothing would conduce so much to the growth and advancement of Burlington as the construction of the Caughnawaga Ship Canal.

INCEPTION OF THE NORTHERN PACIFIC.

While Mr. Canfield was thus engaged in these various enterprises he formed the acquaintance of Mr. Edwin F. Johnson, then perhaps the most experienced railroad engineer in America, who spent much of his time at Burlington in the stone store of Bradley & Canfield. Mr. Johnson, having been projector of the Erie Railroad in 1836 from New York to the lakes, as well as having been engaged in the construction of the Erie canal, had given much thought, and collected from army officers, trappers and traders much information relative to the belt of country between the great lakes and the Pacific ocean, and had become so thoroughly impressed with the importance of a railroad to the Pacific coast that he was constantly talking with Mr. Canfield upon the project to induce him to take hold of it. Mr.

Canfield, who was then about thirty years old, became so much convinced by Mr. Johnson's arguments, as well as by his own study of the country, of the practicability of a railroad across the continent, that he resolved to make it the business of his life and devote his energies and talents to the accomplishment of it, believing he could in no way be so instrumental in promoting the happiness and welfare of his fellow-men as in opening to settlement that immense tract of fertile land in the Northwest, and which would furnish homes for millions of the poor and down-trodden of all nations.

The first active step toward it was the taking of a contract in 1852, by himself and partners, to build the Chicago, St. Paul & Fond du Lac Railroad, now known as the Chicago & Northwestern Railroad, from Chicago to St. Paul, Minnesota, and Fond du Lac, Wisconsin. Mr. Edwin F. Johnson was made chief engineer. At this time there was no railroad into Chicago from the East, and the materials and supplies were transported from Buffalo by boat through the lakes and straits of Mackinac to Chicago. Robert J. Walker, secretary of the treasury of the United States, N. P. Tallmadge, ex-United States senator from New York, and other prominent men were the directors of the company. It was while Mr. Johnson was thus engaged on this road that he used to have long talks with Mr. Canfield about a line of railroad to the Pacific ocean from St. Paul, and wrote an exhaustive treatise upon Pacific railroads, showing that the northern via the Missouri, Yellowstone and Columbia rivers was the most feasible route, as well as passing through the most productive country. This made a volume of 150 pages, with an extended map, which Mr. Canfield and his partner published at their own expense, upon which was traced the isothermal line, showing that the climate became milder from Minnesota to Puget Sound, until a mean temperature there was warmer than Chesapeake Bay.

ORIGIN OF THE THREE PACIFIC RAILROAD EXPEDITIONS.

The Hon. Jefferson Davis at this time was Secretary of war, and with the prominent leaders of the South was very desirous to extend Southern territory, and doubtless had in mind at some future time the acquisition of Mexico. Hearing from his associate in the cabinet, the Hon. Robert J. Walker, that Mr. Johnson had in manuscript the above-mentioned volume, he came to New York and sought an introduction to him, whom he knew to be an engineer of extensive knowledge and that whatever he had written was reliable and important. At his request Mr. Johnson loaned him the manuscript for a few days, and after reading it, and seeing the conclusion to which Mr. Johnson had come, that the northern route was the most feasible, not only with respect to its topographical features, soil, climate and mineral resources, but also of great importance, being so near to the British line in the military and commercial point of view, he came on to New York to return the manuscript and see Mr. Johnson again. Inasmuch as this came in conflict with Mr. Davis' cherished plans, he endeavored to convince Mr. Johnson that he must have greatly underrated the difficulties of the northern route, the obstruction by snow, the elevation of the main summit of the Rocky mountains, which was really 3,000 feet lower than those by the Union Pacific, and that he did not realize how rapidly the ground rises near the source of streams; while to any practical engineer the most feasible point for crossing the Rocky mountains which would naturally strike him, would be at the divide, where the waters of the two rivers to the Pacific ocean and the Gulf of Mexico take their rise—the

Mississippi and Columbia. Mr. Johnson listened attentively to what Mr. Davis had to say and replied: "that he had given the subject much thought and patient investigation, but his conclusions were strictly logical from the facts, and that he had no doubt of the full verification of his estimates by actual measurement hereafter to be made," which the actual surveys for the Northern Pacific Railroad have since confirmed; and if the profile of the Northern Pacific of to-day be compared with the profile accompanying the above manuscript of Mr. Johnson, the coincidence would be found wonderful.

Mr. Davis, finding he could not change Mr. Johnson's views and that Mr. Johnson was going to publish his manuscript, returned to Washington and on the 3d of March, 1853, procured the passage of a resolution by Congress, authorizing him, the Secretary of war, to make such explorations as he might deem advisable, to ascertain the most practicable route for a railroad from the Mississippi river to the Pacific ocean. He at once organized three expeditions, one by the way of the Southern route, one by the middle or Central route, and the other by the Northern route. He placed in charge of the expedition at the eastern end of the Northern route, Major Isaac I. Stevens, then the secretary of the National Democratic Committee, and Lieut. George B. McClellan in charge of the Western end, both of whom were particular friends of his and whom he had expected would probably report unfavorably to the Northern route. In Lieut. McClellan he realized his expectations, but Major Stevens, although entering upon the work with strong prejudices against it, become a convert as he progressed to the Northern route, and fully confirmed all Mr. Johnson had predicted. Major Stevens became so convinced of the superiority of this route that he got the appointment

from President Pierce of the governorship of Washington Territory, and removed there and devoted most of his life in presenting to the public the great importance of this route, and enlightening public opinion with respect to its wonderful resources. To Edwin F. Johnson, more than any other man, at that early day, is due the true presentation to the public of the merits of the Northern Pacific, based upon reliable facts, when there were but very few people in this country who knew anything of its real merits and the resources of the country through which it was to pass; and fewer still who believed it was possible ever to build it. Then and there was inaugurated the first practical steps toward the construction of a railroad by the Northern route in 1852 from Chicago.

In those days railroad building was slow compared with what it is now, materials difficult to get, capital timid, contractors inexperienced, and, before the railroad was finished to Fond du Lac, the panic of 1857 overtook it and stopped all work, embarrassing the company and contractors. Before the company could be reorganized the War of the Rebellion came on, when the urgent necessity of a railroad to the Pacific became apparent, and the Government selected the middle route, or Union Pacific, as the first line to be built, granting it lands and a money subsidy, it being understood at the time that the same money subsidy should at some future time be given to each the Northern and Southern routes. But this was never carried out by Congress, and the railroads by both these routes had to be built by private enterprise, with only the land grant, but without any money subsidy from the United States Government.

MANAGER OF GOVERNMENT RAILROADS DURING
THE WAR OF THE REBELLION.

Soon after the war broke out and the Government assumed control of the railroads of the country, Col. Thomas A. Scott, of the Pennsylvania Railroad, was made assistant secretary of war and general manager, having for his special duties the collecting of the armies of the United States. He sent for Mr. Canfield and placed him in charge of all the railroads about Washington as assistant manager. At this time Washington was surrounded by the rebels, and all communication was cut off, both by land and water, except by the Baltimore & Ohio Railroad, with a single track—all the materials and supplies for the daily support of all the citizens, the army and everything, as well as all passengers and troops, had to be taken over this line. It required from thirty to forty trains a day each way, of about thirty-five cars each, and the fear that the enemy might intercept them at any time caused no little uneasiness to the President and his Cabinet. Even the western end of this road was in the hands of the enemy, its officers and managers, with one honorable exception, the superintendent, William Prescott Smith, were in sympathy and co-operating with the rebels. That portion between Baltimore and Washington was guarded, especially at the culverts, embankments and bridges, by a regiment under the command of Col. John H. Robinson, of Binghamton, New York.

It was a very responsible and trying position. The flower of the Confederate army, under their experienced and popular leader, General Lee, was encamped upon the "sacred soil" in sight of the capitol; rebel spies and allies were everywhere present in disguise, occupying positions of trust in the different departments of the Government, keeping up a constant secret communication with the rebel leaders; the whole North in a state of anxiety and excitement lest the capital of the Union, with its treasures and archives, should fall into the hands of the enemy, while the South was hourly expecting to hear of its surrender to General Lee, and its occupation by their troops.

Every avenue of communication by land and water with the District of Columbia was in the hands of the rebels, except the single iron track to Baltimore, over which the 300,000 soldiers for the Army of the Potomac were to be transported for the defense of Washington, as well as everything for the support of man and beast in and about Washington. It was only after frequent interviews and repeated assurances that Mr. Canfield could satisfy President Lincoln that he could, on the single track, keep open a communication with Washington until the Army of the Potomac should be collected, provided the Government would furnish troops enough to protect the line from destruction.

But the rigid system instituted by Mr. Canfield of guarding the track the whole distance by day and night, the employment of experienced, loyal railroad officers and men whom he knew, and in whom he had confidence; an implicit obedience of all employes to the rules and regulations, enabled him to transport the immense amount of freight, passengers and troops during the whole blockade without an accident of any kind. Never, perhaps, has there been, before or since in this country, so much business done in the same length of time, with so much promptness and safety, upon a single-track railroad. Upon its successful operation the fate of the nation may then have been said to depend. Even after the Army of the Potomac had been collected, had the operation of this railroad been cut off by the rebels, Washington with all its treasures and archives, and even the Army of the Potomac itself, would probably have fallen into the hands of the enemy, the effect of which at that time upon the future of this nation no one can imagine. The recognition of the Southern Confederacy by foreign governments would have been assured, which, together with the small Northern army then in the field and the sympathy of the copperhead element in the North with secession, the preservation of the Union and the suppression of the Rebellion would, to say the least, have been much more difficult. The prevention of such a calamity was due to a great extent to the great experience, untiring watchfulness, cool judgment and careful management of Mr. Canfield, who was master of the situation, keeping his own council as well as the secrets of the Government entrusted to him, so very necessary in those critical times.

Soon after reaching Washington, Mr. Canfield, with the assistance of the Hon. Solomon Foote, senator from Vermont, got permission from Mr. Cameron, secretary of war, to raise a cavalry regiment in Vermont, and within twenty-four hours from the time it was suggested he received a commission for Col. L. B. Platt, of Colchester, with instructions to purchase the horses and raise the regiment at once. As Mr. Canfield could not be spared from Washington, he wrote to leading men in different parts of Vermont, appealing to them to assist, among them Z. H. Canfield, of Arlington, and J. D. Hatch, of Windsor, the result of which was, within sixty days, Col. Platt reported with his regiment at Washington, which rendered service during the war second to no other in the army. The general movement of the army the next season into Virginia and the South raised the blockade and removed the necessity of further vigilance at Washington; and the death of Mr. Doolittle, the superintendent of the steamers on Lake Champlain, created a vacancy which the directors of the company desired Mr. Canfield to fill, which he accepted, returned to Burlington, Vermont, and for several years was the general superintendent and treasurer of the company.

During his superintendency the business of the company increased rapidly, and the few years during his administration were the most prosperous the company ever saw.

In 1865 the Clyde Coal and Mining Company, of Nova Scotia, owned mostly in New York and Pennsylvania, secured his services to go to Cape Breton to open some mines of gas coal, from which place the gas companies of New England, New York and even Washington were supplied. While there Mr. Canfield, in the winter of 1865-66, made an examination of Louisburg Harbor, the best harbor on the Atlantic coast, from Cape North to Cape Sable, thinking it would ultimately become the terminus of the transcontinental railroads, from which point a steamer can make Liverpool in four days. Since that time railroads have been built from the Pacific Ocean to within 100 miles of this place, thus practically confirming his views on the matter.

FORMATION OF THE SYNDICATE TO CONSTRUCT THE NORTHERN PACIFIC RAILROAD.

During the war Josiah Perham, of Maine, had procured a charter from the State of Maine for a railroad from Maine to the Pacific coast, which he called the Peoples' Railroad. His plan was that no person should have more than one share of stock, and that it should never be mortgaged, a purely visionary scheme. Subsequently his friends induced him to abandon it, or in other words, apply to Congress for a new charter with more practical provisions, which, by the assistance of Maj. Isaac I. Stevens, Colonel Aldrich and Senator Henry M. Rice, of Minnesota, and others, he procured under the name of the Northern Pacific. After the war was over he made an attempt to organize it and carry it forward, but his plans were too impracticable, and after spending much time and all his means, as well as some of that of his friends, having issued $600,000 of preferred stock, also, he became discouraged and proposed to transfer the charter and franchise to a foreign party. One of his neighbors, the Hon. R.D. Rice, of Maine, hearing of this, called upon the Hon. J.Gregory Smith, of Vermont, and Benjamin P. Cheney,of Boston, who knew of the value of the franchise, and they arranged with Mr. Perham, the ostensible proprietor, to transfer the whole enterprise to them to save it to this country and from going into the hands of the Grand Trunk Railroad of Canada, which was endeavoring to get control of it. An active man was wanted to take charge of the business, to attend to all the details, to bring the merits of the enterprise before Congress and the country. Mr. Canfield, who was well known to all these gentlemen as having given much attention to the matter in former years, with Mr. Johnson, was appointed a director and general agent of the company, with power to take such measures as he thought necessary to get the company into operation, and to carry out the provisions of the charter in the work of construction, under the advice of the directors from time to time. After the failure of Congress in 1866 and 1867 to grant aid, it was evident that the temper of that body was hostile to further government aid to railroads, which was encouraged by those interested in the Union and Central Pacific Railroads, to prevent, if possible, the building of the northern and southern lines. The directors of the Northern Pacific were much discouraged, and at times were about ready to abandon the enterprise and lose what money they had already put in. But the charter would expire in two years. Mr. Canfield, who had been so many years working for the enterprise, would not consent to give it up without one more effort to save it, knowing full well that with the state of public sentiment then existing, if this charter expired, another would never be granted.

To secure an extension of the charter and give it a more national character than it seemed to have had before, in consequence of most of those identified with it being from New England, Mr. Canfield conceived the idea of a syndicate of gentlemen, to be made up from those occupying prominent positions in the leading railroads of the country. He went to St. Albans and laid the matter before Governor Smith, who was then president of the Northern Pacific Railroad, who concurred in it; but, being too busy with the affairs of the Vermont Central Railroad to give much personal attention to the plan, he told Mr. Canfield to go ahead and he would endorse anything he might do. Mr. Canfield left Burlington for New York on the 26th day of December, 1866, with a heavy heart, but resolved to make a last desperate effort to save the magnificent enterprise about which he had already spent so many years of his life. Mr. William B. Ogden, of Chicago, with whom Mr. Canfield had long been acquainted, was the president of the Chicago & Northwestern Railroad, was better informed upon the resources of the great Northwest, and had spent more time in investigating them than any other man of his time, and could better appreciate the magnitude of the Northern Pacific and the development of an empire which must follow its construction. Mr. Canfield felt that his first point was to secure the active co-operation of Mr. Ogden and induce him to take hold of it, notwithstanding he was overwhelmed with business.

It was some days before he could get Mr. Ogden to give any attention to it; but finally secured an appointment with him to spend a day at his home at Boscobel, near High Bridge, twelve miles from New York, and take up the subject.

Mr. Canfield, early on the day appointed, went to Boscobel with his maps, plans and printed copies of the charter, and commencing with its provisions and discussing them, he soon enlisted the interest of Mr. Ogden to such an extent that they continued their discussion from 9 o'clock in the morning until midnight. Mr. Canfield's plan was to form a syndicate of twelve men, representing the leading railway, express and transportation interests of the country, and to give to each one-twelfth of the enterprise, they paying therefor their proportion of the original cost. Thus the twelve would own the enterprise, each subscriber coming in on the "ground floor." The twelve names presented by Mr. Canfield were acceptable to Mr. Ogden.

During this interview at Boscobel, in considering the various questions and emergencies which might arise in the unknown future before the road should be "put upon its feet," and the work of construction commenced, Mr. Ogden said to Mr. Canfield, "How much money will it require to bring this about? how much money will each one have to pay, and how long will it take?"

Mr. Canfield frankly replied, "that it was a long road to travel, that it had bitter and strong enemies in and out of Congress to contend with, and that you, Mr. Ogden, with your experience, know that it would take considerable money to make surveys and do preliminary work upon so long a route across the Rocky mountains, of which each one is expected to furnish his proportion from time to time."

"What then," said Mr. Ogden, "will be the chance of our getting our money back?"

"About one in fifty," said Mr. Canfield.

"A fine chance," said Mr. Ogden; "and upon what ground then, Mr. Canfield, do you ask us to put up our money, with so little prospect of return?"

"Upon this ground, Mr. Ogden, which I have no doubt will commend itself to your good judgment: This enterprise is one of the greatest ever undertaken in the world — it is equal to that of the East India Company — it is the only continuous charter ever granted across this continent, from water to water, and with the prevailing sentiment, which is increasing in this country, of hostility to railroad grants, assisted by Government aid of subsidy, or even wild lands, if this is allowed to lapse, another will never be granted; it will open up an empire, now occupied by the savages, which will furnish happy homes for millions of the poor of this and other countries, and the resources and wealth which it will develop will simply be incalculable; and withal it will be the great highway for the trade of China, Japan and the East Indies, across the continent. It is due to the people of this country and to this nation, that you, gentlemen, whom Providence has placed at the head of the great transportation interests of the country, should step in at this crisis and use your influence and advance your money to save this magnificent enterprise from destruction."

"And suppose I put my money in for such a laudable purpose, what have you got to give me or others who may be associated with us to show for it?"

"I have nothing to give. I have suggested the names of twelve men, including ourselves," said Mr. Canfield, "whom I believe to be honorable men, and whose word, once given, will serve every purpose."

"I suppose it is, then," said Mr. Ogden, "simply a matter of honor between gentlemen."

"Exactly."

"Well, Mr. Canfield, that is high and noble ground. The charter must be saved and I will take hold with you. Meet me at my office, 57 Broadway, to-morrow morning, and we will lay siege to the directors of the Chicago & Northwestern Railroad, whose influence we must enlist." So saying, Mr. Ogden rang his bell for his coachman and directed him to drive Mr. Canfield to the Fifth Avenue Hotel.

It was past midnight, and Mr. Canfield retired much lighter-hearted than when he left Vermont, and feeling that a good day's work had been done, and that daylight was about to dawn upon his favorite project.

In order that there should be no cause for disagreement in the future and that the objects for which the syndicate was formed should be distinctly understood, as up to this time Mr. Canfield had made only a rough sketch of them, he telegraphed to Vermont to Governor Smith to come to New York, and with him spent most of the 10th day of January, 1867, at the Fifth Avenue Hotel, in putting on to paper in a condensed form the agreement for the twelve parties to sign, which was really the Constitution upon which was based the future proceedings and which was afterwards known in the affairs of the company as the "Original Interests Agreement." It was late in the afternoon when they took this document to 57 Broadway to submit to Mr. Ogden, which, after discussion and explanation, received his hearty approval without a single alteration. It was getting dark, and as Mr. Ogden had to drive to his home at Boscobel, twelve miles, he said:

"Well, gentlemen, is there anything else to do?"

"Yes, there is one thing more," said Mr. Canfield, "that is, for you to take the pen and put your name to this paper for one of the one-twelfth interests."

"But it is so dark," said Mr. Ogden, "I do not know as I can see to write, and if I do, as you can read it."

"Well," said Mr. Canfield, "try it and we will accept the signature for better or worse." Mr. Ogden then signed his name and they separated. As Governor Smith and Mr. Canfield walked up Broadway, passing Trinity church, Governor Smith said he felt that a critical turning-point in the Northern Pacific enterprise had been passed and that that signature fixed the star of the Northern Pacific.

Mr. Canfield and the Governor soon after procured the remaining signatures to the agreement, which composed the syndicate, as follows: J. Gregory Smith, of St. Albans, Vermont, president of the Central Vermont Railroad; Richard D. Rice, of Augusta, Maine, president of the Maine Central Railroad; Thomas H. Canfield, of Burlington, Vermont; William B. Ogden, of Chicago, Illinois, president of the Chicago & Northwestern Railroad; Robert H. Berdell, of New York, president of the Erie Railroad; Danforth N. Barney, of New York, president of Wells, Fargo & Co., Express Company; Ashbel H. Barney, New York, president of United States Express Company; Benjamin P. Cheney, of Boston, president of United States & Canada Express Company; William G. Fargo, of Buffalo, New York, vice-president of New York Central Railroad and president of the American Express Company; George W. Cass, of Pittsburgh, Pennsylvania, president Pittsburgh, Fort Wayne & Chicago Railroad; J. Edgar Thompson, of Philadelphia, Pa., president of the Pennsylvania Railroad; and Edward Reilley, of Lancaster, Pennsylvania. At a later day a division of some of these interests was made by which Jay Cooke & Co., Charles B. Wright, Thomas A. Scott, of Philadelphia; Frederick Billings, of Woodstock, Vermont, and William Windom and William S. King, of Minnesota, became actively interested, the two latter gentlemen being the only men from Minnesota, except Governor Ramsey and Mr. Donnelly, who manifested at that day any great interest in the undertaking, and the only men from that State who advanced any money to help along the enterprise. Strange does it seem that the citizens of a State which it was evident then must receive, and since has received, so much benefit from this railroad, should not have taken more interest in promoting it, when it needed the most assistance in its dark days, and when men from the East who had not a dollar of property in Minnesota were devoting their time and money to organize and put into operation this magnificent undertaking.

And at this day it seems hardly possible to believe that all the delegation in Congress from Illinois except General Logan and Norman B. Judd; from Indiana except Governor Morton, Daniel Voorhees and M. C. Morton; from Ohio except Senator Sherman and two or three others, should have opposed it in Congress, and that such men as E. B. Washburn, John Wentworth and Columbus Delano should fight it bitterly on the floor for many days, and finally defeated any aid of any kind, either in subsidy of bonds or guarantee of interest.

Six of the former directors resigned, and Messrs. Ogden, Cass, Thompson, Berdell, Fargo and Canfield were elected in their places.

SURVEYS AND EXPLORATIONS.

The new board found it necessary, in order to satisfy the numerous inquiries made in Congress as to the practicability of the route, and in order to fix a definite location, to institute surveys from Lake Superior going west and from Puget Sound coming east. In order to do this Edwin F. Johnson was chosen chief engineer, and Thomas H. Canfield general manager to collect funds, make disbursements and attend generally to the business of the company. Thus the two men who, in 1852, so often laid plans for a Pacific railroad in the "stone store" at Burlington, Vermont, were, after fifteen years, brought together again as the active men in starting forward and taking charge of this great enterprise.

Gen. Ira Spaulding was detailed as assistant engineer of the Minnesota division, with instructions to run a line from Bayfield, Wisconsin, to St. Cloud, Minnesota, thence via Sauk Centre and Alexandria, keeping south of the Leaf Hills, to some point on the Red River near Georgetown; and another line from Superior, Wisconsin, in charge of M. C. Kimberly (now assistant manager of the road), via French Rapids (now near Brainerd), Leaf River and Detroit Lake, to intercept the other line, which was done, making the point of intersection on the south branch of the Buffalo river, about two miles west of Glyndon. At that time it was the expectation that the road would run north of the Missouri river, via Devil's Lake, Fort Benton and Cadott's Pass, to Missoula, although the route via the Yellowstone was under consideration, and which was finally adopted, crossing the Rocky mountains at Mullan Pass to Missoula. The point of divergence of the Yellowstone route from the upper Missouri route was at the west end of the cut, two miles east of Audubon. Gen. James Tilton, of Delaware, who was the Government engineer appointed by President Pierce to establish the Willamette meridian and to survey the original townships in Oregon and Washington Territory, was employed on account of his familiarity with that country to examine the Cascade mountains, which presented the most formidable barrier to the passage of a railroad. His examination determined the existence of at least three or four practicable passes in the Cascade range, viz.: Packwoods or the Cowlitz, south of Mount Tacoma, leading from the Cowlitz river on the west to the Atahnam branch of the Yakima river on the east; another, the Snoqualmie pass, north of Mount Tacoma to Lake Kitchelas, a tributary of the Yakima; and Cady's pass, still farther north, between the waters of the We-nach-ee and Skykomish. Since that time a fourth one has been discovered between the Snoqualmie and Mount Tacoma, the Stampede pass, through which the railroad now runs.

As there were hardly any settlements or roads then through the country where these lines passed, and the only way to reach the Pacific coast being by Panama and the Isthmus, consequently, so soon after the war closed, when gold was 175 to 200, the expenses of all preliminary surveys or work over a country of thousands of miles, so inaccessible for ordinary transportation, many of the supplies having to be carried in upon the backs of horses and in some cases by Indians, became very great, and at times it seemed almost impossible to carry on the work at all. At the same time, while these surveys and other explorations were being made, its enemies were at work with Congress to prevent an extension of its charter, destroy its land grant, and defeat a money subsidy, such as had been given to the Union Pacific. To accomplish this, strong inducements were offered by powerful parties for a surrender of the west end of the line from Montana to Puget Sound to competing routes, coupled with the assurance that with such surrender their assistance would be given to secure a subsidy for the whole line, but without such surrender they would defeat it. Tempting as such a proposition was financially, in the straitened circumstances of the company, yet it was spurned with contempt by the officers, and Mr. Canfield gave the party making it to understand, that it was the only continuous charter that ever was or probably ever would be granted across the continent, and that under no circumstances or emergency, however pressing, would the promoters submit to its dismemberment, subsidy or no subsidy, and that the railroad would be built as a continuous, unbroken, transcontinental line, under its charter, intact and unimpaired, from the Great Lakes to the Pacific Ocean.

The result has been that the promise of the party was fulfilled, and the subsidy was defeated; while that of Mr. Canfield has also been fulfilled, and the Northern Pacific Railroad has been built from Lake Superior to Puget Sound with its charter unimpaired. Too much credit can not be given to the promoters for taking their strong stand against dismemberment in those stormy days.

Notwithstanding all these difficulties, in addition to numerous others which the limits of this article will not permit to be mentioned, the subscribers to the syndicate continued cheerfully to make advances for the cost of surveys and other expenses of the company until they had furnished about a quarter of a million of dollars from their own private pockets, and until the company was fairly under way by the financial arrangement with Jay Cooke & Co., Mr. Canfield in the meantime receiving all the moneys, making the disbursements, keeping the accounts until they were turned over to the new organization, arising from the arrangement with Messrs. Cooke & Co., and the original twelve parties to the syndicate relieved from their personal obligations. During the whole of this time not a member of the syndicate hesitated for a moment when called upon for his proportion, nor entertained a doubt as to the ultimate results of the undertaking.

To those of the present day who pass over this beautiful, diversified country of 2,000 miles, from Lake Superior to Puget Sound, at the rate of forty miles per hour, in the elegant palace cars of the Northern Pacific Railroad Company, through flourishing villages and cities, amid the golden wheat fields of Minnesota and Dakota, the rich mines, and flocks and "herds upon a thousand hills" in Montana and Idaho, and the magnificent forests of Washington Territory, it is impossible by any language to convey to them an idea of the innumerable trials, the almost insuperable difficulties and insurmountable obstacles which surrounded this enterprise for two or three years, even before a bar of iron was laid, not to mention those which the panic of 1873 entailed upon it. *But for the advances, courage, faith and influence of these twelve men, there would have been no Northern Pacific Railroad to-day.* Those were the dark days of the enterprise, when it required faith and courage, when the project was ridiculed as impossible, and its advocates as crazy and visionary ; and in view of the ignorance which then pervaded the whole country as to the climate, resources and practicability of this route to the Pacific, and the consequent obloquy and ridicule which was poured out upon those who had undertaken it, it is safe to say that at least as much credit is due to those twelve men who, amid good and evil report, stood up with their brains and money and carried it through, as to those in later days, who, after its practicability had been demonstrated, confidence created; money raised and success assured, have been instrumental in its final completion.

Mr. Canfield spent much time in Washington at different times to secure the necessary legislation for extending the charter of the company, procuring the right to mortgage, and the right to build from Portland to Puget Sound as well as resisting the repeated attacks upon the land grant. Inasmuch as section 10 of the original charter prohibited the company from making any mortgage or issuing any bonds, without which it would be impossible to construct such a road, Mr. Canfield went in the winter of 1868–69 to Washington, and by the assistance of Senator Edmunds, of Vermont, and others, got an amendment to the charter passed, authorizing the company to issue bonds and secure the same by mortgage, for the purpose of raising funds to build the railroad. At the extra session of Congress called by President Grant in March, 1869, for one month, he also got through an act extending the branch line

from Portland to Puget Sound, upon which was the first iron laid by the company, which has proved to be an important link in its chain, connecting, as it does, Oregon and Washington Territory.

THE CHARTER ALMOST LOST TWICE.

But for Mr. Canfield's vigilance the company would have lost its charter in 1866, and again in 1868. The jealousy of the Union Pacific, which by the aid of the Government subsidy had been constructed, as well as that of the Southern Pacific, developed a strong indication that it would require considerable work at Washington to save the life of the infant Northern Pacific. They would not consent to an extension of over two years, while it should have been ten years for such an enterprise. Upon the first opportunity, which soon came up, Col. Thomas A. Scott, an old friend, who was interested in the Southern Pacific, had gotten his bill reported by the railroad committee, and all ready to bring up in the House for an extension of his charter on the next Monday morning, as soon as the House should be called to order, before many of the members should get there, except his own friends, who understood what was to be done.

Mr. Canfield went to him and wanted him to allow a short section to be added to his bill, extending the time of the Northern Pacific. He would not consent, but said, "Pass mine first and then I will have my friends take hold and pass yours." While friends of the Northern Pacific would and did vote for his, they could not rely upon his Southern men to go for a Northern route—and dared not try the experiment. After Congress adjourned on Saturday, Mr. Canfield went over to Mr. Stevens, better known in those days as "Uncle Thad" (who, by the way, with Senator Jacob Howard, of Michigan, the chairman of the Pacific Railroad committee in the Senate, known as "Honest

Jake," were both natives of Vermont, the former from Peacham, in Caledonia county, and the latter from Shaftsbury, Bennington county, and were both warm friends of the Northern Pacific), and told him his interview with Colonel Scott. "Ha! ha!" said he, "don't be troubled, I will take care of Thomas A. You see Speaker Colfax and tell him I want to be recognized Monday morning when Thomas' bill is called up."

Monday morning came. As soon as the speaker's gavel fell, Scott's man called up his bill and at once the shrill voice of "Uncle Thad" was heard, "Mr. Speaker, I offer the following amendment, which the clerk will please read—'and be it further resolved, that the time for commencing and completing the Northern Pacific railroad and all its several sections is extended for the term of two years.'"

No one dared oppose Uncle Thad.

"Those in favor of the amendment," said the speaker, "will say aye, and those opposed, no; the ayes have it, and the amendment is adopted. Those in favor of the bill as amended will say aye; opposed will say no; the bill is passed." There was not an opposition vote, and all was done quicker than this is written. Thus the child's life was prolonged two years, until July 2, 1868. Had it not been for this maneuvering and watchfulness, it is most likely the charter would have expired, as it was impossible in the state of feeling then existing to have got enough Southern members with the friends of the Northern Pacific to have passed it.

At this time, also, a bill was before Congress asking the guarantee of interest on the bonds of the company, as it had become satisfied that it was useless to attempt to get a subsidy, as the Union Pacific had done. To show the great benefits to the nation, Mr. Canfield conferred with General Grant, General Meigs, quartermaster-general, General Ingalls and other officers of the army,

who had been stationed many years on the Northwestern coast, and procured their views with respect to the Northern Pacific, all of whom, in every aspect of the case, deemed it a matter of great importance to the nation. General Meigs, in his communication, says: "The construction of the road will make the now wild and waste regions through which it is to pass centers of national wealth and production and military strength, and from the mountains themselves a hardy population will pour down upon the coast, at every hostile demonstration. A guarantee of a fixed rate of interest upon the cost of construction is a mode of assistance to their great enterprises, now common in the heavily taxed countries of Europe. If those governments, burdened with the immense annual expenditure of standing armies, almost as large in times of peace as we have been compelled to support in time of war, find it in the interest of their revenues thus to aid free travel and transport through countries already provided with navigable rivers and excellent wagon roads, we may confidently assume that our country will find ample reward for any such expenditure in opening up a highway for fraternal intercourse between our older communities on the Atlantic and the rising settlements on the Pacific coast; a highway to which the inevitable laws of commerce will attract the trade of the East. The trade of China, Japan and India, a trade along whose slow and painful track, when it was conducted by beasts of burden and by oars and sails instead of the iron horse and ocean steamship, great cities sprung up in the desert sands of Asia and on the coast of the Mediterranean, Babylon, Nineveh, Palmyra, Bagdad, Damascus, Constantinople, Alexandria, Rome, Venice, Geneva and London, the outgrowths of this trade in former centuries. The lines of Pacific railway will found such cities in the new, healthful and inviting regions through which its eastern flow is destined to enrich the world; and Oregon as well as California, Montana as well as Utah, will hereafter have their San Franciscos, Chicagos, St. Louises, Cincinnatis, great emporia of an internal commerce heretofore unknown, as well as the world-encircling commerce of the Indies."

General Grant sent the following:

Headquarters Armies of the United States, }
April 20, 1866. }

The construction of a railroad by the proposed route would be of very great advantage to the Government pecuniarily by saving us the cost of transportation to supply troops whose presence in the country through which it is proposed to pass is made necessary by the great amount of emigration to the gold-bearing regions of the Rocky mountains. In my opinion, too, the United States would receive an additional pecuniary benefit in the construction of this road by the settlement it would induce along the line of the road, and consequently the less number of troops necessary to secure order and safety. How far these benefits should be compensated by the General Government beyond the grant of lands already awarded by Congress, I would not pretend to say. I would merely give it as my opinion that the enterprise of constructing the Northern Pacific Railroad is one well worth fostering by the General Government, and that such aid could well be afforded as would insure the early prosecution of the work.   U. S. GRANT,
Lieutenant-General.

But two years soon passed away, and meanwhile the Northern Pacific began to attract considerable attention, as well as to increase the hostility of the Union and Southern Pacific towards it. But after about four months' hard work another bill was passed by the House and concurred in by the Senate on the 28th day of June, while the charter expired on the 2d day of July. The bill had been returned from the Senate, reported to the House, engrossed and passed over to the committee on enrolled bills, of which Mr. Holman was chairman, to be taken to the President for his signature. Mr. Canfield, finding the bill did not reach the White House as it should, and as there was but a day or two left, became very nervous and uneasy, as well as unable to find Mr. Holman, who had taken charge of the bill. In this emergency he consulted with Messrs. Windom and Woodbridge, members of the House, and they went to the speaker, Mr. Colfax, who ordered the desk of Mr. Holman to be opened, and there found the bill, and gave it to another member of the committee to take to the White House. It is supposed Mr. Holman was sick somewhere and had forgotten about it. But for this watchfulness on the part of Mr. Canfield, the Northern Pacific charter might have slept the sleep of death in the desk of its worst enemy in the House. *It was signed by the President July 1st, only one day before the charter expired.*

To most people it would seem that an enterprise which was to confer so much benefit upon mankind—which was really to dispense with the necessity of an army to keep the Indian tribes in subjection—which was to open up the millions of acres of wild lands of the Government, furnishing a market for them, which were heretofore worthless, to industrious and hardy settlers and thereby increase the wealth of the nation, would receive attention from Congress and an act to facilitate its operation be passed without delay. But such is not the case. Opposition arises in unexpected quarters; secret combinations are formed; jealousies and sectional interests turn up which ought not to have any bearing upon such an important subject, all of which would require close attention in order to carry through legislation of even meritorious character. Truly the ways of Congress "are past finding out," especially to the uninitiated.

FINANCIAL ARRANGEMENT WITH JAY COOKE & CO.

Mr. Canfield was one of the committee, consisting of Messrs. Smith, Ogden and Rice, who went to Ogontz, Mr. Cooke's country residence, near Philadelphia, in May, 1869, to make the arrangement with Jay Cooke & Co. to negotiate the bonds of the Northern Pacific Railroad. After spending a day or two and finally agreeing to the terms of the arrangement, just as the committee were leaving, supposing all things were done, Mr. Cooke proposed a condition, as a postscript to the agreement, that the agreement should not be binding upon him, unless by a personal examination by himself or his agents, of the whole line, it should be shown to be equal to all the representations as to resources and practicability which the directors had made. This Mr. Cooke insisted upon, even if it should take a year to do it.

Mr. Canfield was very much annoyed by this unexpected demand of Mr. Cooke, fearing that it would so delay the commencement of construction, which had already been made the basis of objections before Congress to any further extension of charter, and he remonstrated with Mr. Cooke, explaining to him the dangers of further delay.

Mr. Cooke replied, " that so far as he was concerned, he was entirely satisfied with all the directors had represented about the practicability of the line, the wonderful resources of the country through which it was to pass and the great benefit to the nation, but that he had to engage bankers all over this country and Europe to assist him in placing the bonds, that capital was timid, that thousands of questions would arise which we could not anticipate, and that to answer them satisfactorily it was necessary he should be able to say that his own experts had examined the whole country, and that his information was based upon their examinations and not upon the reports of any one identified with the road, and that in the long run it would be seen his condition would be for the benefit of the enterprise."

Mr. Ogden, perceiving that Mr. Canfield was annoyed, called him one side and said: " I think you are a little vexed with Mr. Cooke."

" Yes, I confess," said Mr. Canfield, "I am a little mad, after we have spent so much time to make an agreement, now not only to have it upset, but to have all our plans endangered before Congress."

" But," said Mr. Ogden, " I have been two years endeavoring to negotiate a loan for the Northwestern Railroad of only $4,000,000 secured upon a road of 1,000 miles, now in operation through a rich and prosperous country, while this man proposes to negotiate $100,000,000 upon a line through an unknown country and not a bar of iron laid yet. You must remember no negotiation of such a magnitude has ever been undertaken in the history of the world under such circumstances, and while he may not be able or live to entirely complete it, yet if he only negotiates part of it, it will put us on our feet and ultimately secure the construction of the Northern Pacific Railroad, and we can not afford now to break up our contract with him."

" Well," said Mr. Canfield, " I appreciate as fully as you do the force of your argument, as well as the importance Mr. Cooke attaches to this proposed exploration which will delay us six months more, but I accede to it, and now let us get about it at once and be done with it before Congress meets in December."

The wisdom of Mr. Ogden's theory has been demonstrated since in the raising of money to build the road.

One can well imagine why a man of action like Mr. Canfield should have been annoyed at a delay of six months more in the work, after he had been for years struggling with opposition, rebuff and difficulties of all kinds, in order to reach a point, where, at least, he had hoped to show to the world by actual work of construction that the Northern Pacific was something besides a railroad on paper. Mr. Canfield was selected by the directors to take charge of Mr. Cooke's party, consisting of W. Milnor Roberts, engineer; Samuel Wilkeson, since Secretary of the Company, William G. Moorehead, Jr., the Rev. Dr. Claxton, and William Johnson, a son of the chief engineer, which was to meet him at Salt Lake City on the 14th of June, 1869.

EXPLORATION FOR THE LINE IN WASHINGTON AND MONTANA TERRITORIES.

From there they went by the Central Pacific Railroad to Sacramento and Marysville, and then by stage through Northern California and Oregon, 700 miles, to Portland, Oregon, arriving there on the 4th of July, 1869. From there they went to Puget Sound —most of the way by stage—procured a small steamer, making a thorough examination of all the bays, towns and harbors, and, returning to Portland, they went by steamer up the Columbia river to Walla Walla, which was about the end of all settlements, and where for some years had been a Government military post. They were now about to enter upon an unknown country, where there were only scattering settlers for a short distance; no roads, no bridges nor any means of subsistence. When on Puget Sound an amusing incident occurred. George Francis Train, who was at Portland to deliver the Fourth of July oration, accompanied the party to the Sound, and when at Whatcom, on Bellingham Bay, he telegraphed to the mayor of Victoria, British Columbia, that he would be there the next day to deliver a lecture, subject, "The downfall of England! get out your guns!" The steamer with the party arrived at Victoria about 3 o'clock the next morning and anchored. When daylight came a man-of-war lay off-side a few rods with her "guns out" and shotted, ready for action. The party were not allowed to land, and it was with much difficulty Mr. Canfield,

with the aid of the American consul, persuaded the officials of Victoria that Mr. Train was a harmless man, and that his message was intended as a joke. But poor Train had insulted Johnny Bull and was not permitted to go ashore after all.

A HORSEBACK EXPEDITION ACROSS THE MOUNTAINS.

At Walla Walla Mr. Canfield fitted out a horseback expedition, consisting of thirteen saddle and pack-horses, and as there were no settlements of any consequence beyond Walla Walla, was obliged to take provisions and cooking utensils upon the backs of his horses, sufficient to last the party thirty days, which it was estimated would bring them to Helena, Montana, 500 miles. Their supplies were confined to tea, coffee, ham, flour, butter, a few canned goods, the long distance preventing the transportation of vegetables or other kinds of meat. Everything had to be in the most condensed form. They left Walla Walla on the 20th of July, 1869, with the thermometer 110 degrees above zero, making about twenty miles a day, lying upon the ground at night without any tent to cover them. They went from Walla Walla to Kentuck's Crossing on the Snake river; thence to Hangman's creek, Schnebley's bridge, near where Spokane Falls now is—then but one log cabin. From there to Pend d'Oreille Lake. Here they found a small steamer, "Mary Moody," which had been used in former mining days, but now dismantled. To save a journey of several days around the lake, they put the engine together and took their horses across the lake on the steamer to the foot of Cabinet Rapids. Here they disembarked, and, following Clark's fork of the Columbia river, crossing many of the mountain ranges at an altitude of several thousand feet to Thompson's Falls, Horse Plains, along the Flathead and Jocko rivers, through the Coriacen Defile to Missoula, thence along the Blackfoot to Gold creek; now near Garrison's, where they made a detour through the Deer Lodge valley to examine the Deer Lodge pass. They went over to the Wisdom river, one of the tributaries of the Jefferson, by very easy grade, and which they found to be the easiest pass in the mountains, and which Mr. Canfield advised as the true route for the road to take, following, after crossing the mountains, the waters of the Jefferson to Gallatin valley, and which he still believes will be the route sooner or later adopted for the through business; although in order to reach Helena, the capital of Montana, the road has been built through the Mullan pass. There were but two or three miners' shanties then at Silver Bow, and the city of Butte, now with 20,000 people, then "was not." Returning to Gold creek, the first place gold was discovered in Montana, they crossed the Rocky mountains to Helena at Mullan's pass, where the railroad tunnel now is. Here they disbanded their horses and took stages to Fort Benton, examining Cadotte's pass on their return, which was the pass Governor Stevens and his expedition crossed in 1854.

AN INDIAN OUTBREAK.

Here they met an Indian outbreak, in which Malcolm Clark, a graduate of West Point and for many years a Government agent, met his death, which threatened much danger, their horses being stolen from them by the Indians at Dearborn river. Soon after leaving Helena, Mr. Canfield received a message from Cadotte, then at Fort Benton, that "North Star," a celebrated chief with a band of 50 warriors was on his way South and would be at Dearborn river on the next day and that he had better look out for him, and it was probably his band which stole his horses. It was a critical time, as General De Trobriand, who was in command

at Fort Shaw, some thirty miles beyond, where they arrived at eight o'clock that evening, refused to give them any assistance. It was very important that Cadotte pass should be examined, inasmuch as it would probably be the place of crossing the main range of the Rockies, if the road went north of the Missouri river. Mr. Canfield, at Fort Benton, endeavored to get Cadotte himself to pilot them over it, as he had done General Stevens in 1854, but his fear of being massacred by the Indians made him refuse absolutely to accompany them, however great the inducements offered. The probable reason why Cadotte would not accompany the party was, that the Indians are particularly hostile to half-breeds who act as guides to the whites through their country, and will shoot them at sight, and hence, as there was an uprising of the Indians, he dare not risk his life as a guide for the party, and perhaps it was as well he did not, as it might have caused the Indians to attack them. Mr. Canfield then returned to Fort Shaw, and, after much urging, induced General De Trobriand to give them an escort of six men, really of no use in case of an attack. Fortunately, however, none was made, and they crossed the pass over the mountains and back, and returned to Helena without injury. At Helena and Deer Lodge he was warmly welcomed by the citizens, as being the first director of a railroad who had ever visited Montana, and to them the harbinger of brighter days. From Helena they went to Bozeman, crossing at the Three Forks, where Madison, Gallatin and Jefferson rivers meet, and form the Missouri.

BROUGHT TO A STOP BY "SITTING BULL."

Here a consultation was held with Colonel Brackett, in command of Fort Ellis, near Bozeman, General Sully, the old Indian fighter, and General De Trobriand, who had in the meantime come down from

Fort Shaw, as to the expediency of continuing their expedition down the Yellowstone river to Fort Buford, or across from Glendive to where Bismarck now is located. Although the Crow Indians, whose reservation was about 200 miles east, were friendly, yet Sitting Bull and his band of Sioux, who were encamped about the Big Horn, Tongue and Powder rivers, was not friendly, but upon the other hand, hostile. The officers decided that it would be simply impossible for them, with all the troops at their command, to escort the party through the Sioux territory safely, and advised Mr. Canfield to abandon the expedition without going any further east. There still were the Bozeman mountains, which had not been examined, and which it would be necessary to cross in case the Yellowstone line should be adopted, and Mr. Canfield determined at all hazards to cross them to the Yellowstone, if no further. He accordingly raised a few men and horses at Bozeman, and went over the pass to a point where Livingston now is. Here they remained for a day, and as the rest of the route to the east was by the valley, the Yellowstone, where there were no serious obstacles, and as all that part between here and the Pacific ocean, about one thousand miles, where were all the mountains and difficult parts of the route had been carefully examined, and passes found which would admit of a railroad being built, the representatives of Mr. Cooke decided their mission had practically been accomplished ; and assuring Mr. Canfield that their declining to go down the Yellowstone Valley would not affect the substance of their report, he returned to Bozeman. Mr. Canfield then turned back with his party, went across the country with a mule team 150 miles to Virginia City, and took stages to Corrinne, and then by the Union Pacific Railroad to the East, reaching New York after an absence of about three months. During the trip the engineers had been very reticent as to their views of the route, which created no little anxiety on the part of Mr. Canfield, lest they might not make a favorable report. This was a very important matter to the company at this time, as upon the report of these men Mr. Cooke would furnish the money or not to go on with the construction. Mr. Canfield felt that a great responsibility was placed upon him, as in the event of his not showing them a good route, such as would be satisfactory, the whole arrangement with Mr. Cooke must be abandoned, as well as the construction of the road. But Mr. Canfield, by his study of the route in former years—from the information he had obtained from prominent and intelligent settlers in Oregon, Washington and Montana, and officers of the army—was enabled to conduct the expedition through a favorable route, which subsequent surveys have confirmed, and the railroad from the Columbia river to the Yellowstone has been finally built on the route he reported and most of the way in sight of the very trail which this party made in 1869. The result of the expedition turned out favorably, and the gentlemen sent on by Mr. Cooke unanimously reported that the half had not been told by the directors, and that the country was in fact far better than they had ever represented it to be.

In the meantime Mr. Cooke's party, which had been sent out from St. Paul under the charge of Governor Smith and Mr. Rice, two of the directors, to explore and examine the eastern end of the line from Lake Superior to the Missouri river, had returned and reported very favorably upon their part, which complied fully with the condition required by Mr. Cooke in the postscript to the agreement, much to his satisfaction, and he at once commenced negotiating the bonds, and the work of construction began.

Thus, after nearly four years of continuous struggle by the syndicate, they had reached the great turning point of the commencement of construction of their cherished undertaking.

ORGANIZATION OF THE LAKE SUPERIOR AND PUGET SOUND COMPANY.

It was soon found that many of the crossings of rivers and other places favorable to the location of towns were upon even sections, while the company, under their grant from Congress, received only the odd ones, and had no right under their charter to buy lands. In order to get over this difficulty a company was formed called "The Lake Superior & Puget Sound Company," of which Mr. Canfield was made president, which was empowered to buy lands, build boats, and do most any kind of business to further the interest of the railroad company. In carrying out the plans contemplated by the Lake Superior & Puget Sound Company, Mr. Canfield located, platted and laid out on the line of the Northern Pacific Railroad, between Lake Superior and the Red river, the towns of Komoka, Kimberly, Aitkin, Brainerd, Motley, Aldrich, Wadena, Perham, Audubon, Lake Park, Hawley, Glyndon and Moorhead.

In 1870, when the only railroad north or west of St. Paul was the one to Sauk Rapids, Mr. Canfield and Governor Smith came up from there by team to old Crow Wing and stopped with old Captain Beaulieu, now living at White Earth, which was the end of white settlement in that direction. They then went up the Mississippi river to find a place where there were two high banks that the road could cross without the necessity of a draw-bridge, and selected the place where Brainerd now is, and, at the same time, selected the place for the shops also the station and headquarters. This was then a wilderness, and Mr. Canfield at once surveyed the tract and laid out what is the present city of Brainerd, and placed Lyman P. White in charge as agent, who has filled the position ever since, Mrs. White being the first white woman to live in Brainerd. Engineers then proceeded to locate the railroad east and west from this place. The next year, when the track had been laid about eighteen miles west of Brainerd, Mr. Canfield, in company with several directors of the road and others, made a trip into Dakota, with Pierre Bottineau for a guide, who is still living near Red Lake Falls. They had to carry their provisions with them, both for man and beast. From the end of the track they passed through the woods, encamping the first night west of the Crow Wing river, a few miles north of Aldrich, and the second night at Otter Tail lake. Here they found a few huts which had been occupied previous to the Indian outbreak in 1862. Thence they went across the prairie south of Perham, crossing the Otter Tail where the railroad now does, also at Frazee City, then through woods on the banks of Detroit lake, and camping that night on the banks of the lake near where Detroit now is. There was but one house at Detroit, and that a log one built by Mr. Tyler. Thence to Audubon, the next day striking Sand Beach lake where Mr. Boyer now lives and through the woods to the north side of Lake Flora, on which Lake Park is now located. Here they stopped for lunch. They were particularly pleased with the surrounding scenery, and all thought that this was the most beautiful country they had ever seen. Mr. Martin Olson had just got here a few days before in a "prairie schooner" with his family and took up a claim on Lake La Belle, where he still resides. The party encamped that night on the high ground beyond Muskoda, in full view of the Red River Valley. Next morning, while the most of the party moved on toward the Red

river, Mr. Canfield took four or five of the
directors across the Buffalo and went on to
where Moorhead and Fargo now are, to
show them the place he had selected for these
towns and the crossing of the Red river, and
in the afternoon went down the river, joining the rest of the party at Georgetown, the Hudson Bay post, the only settlement in that part of the country. The next
day—Sunday—was spent at Georgetown, on
the Dakota side of the river, where religious
services were held. There being no clergy-
man with the party, Dr. Samuel W. Thayer,
of Burlington, Vermont, the medical director
of the company, read the services of the
Episcopal Church, assisted by Mr. Canfield,
in which all the party joined heartily, and
especially in the psalms and hymns; con-
spicuous in their strong voices were Vice-
President Colfax, Messrs. Ogden, Billings
and Nettleton. The party consisted of Governor Smith, of Vermont, president of
the Northern Pacific Railroad; Frederick
Billings, of Woodstock, Vermont; W. B.
Ogden, of Chicago; A. H. Barney, of
New York; Richard D. Rice, of Maine;
William Windom, of Minnesota, and Thomas
H. Canfield, all directors; Dr. S. W. Thayer,
Hon. Schuyler Colfax, Gen. A. B. Nettleton and George B. Wright, of Minneapolis;
C. Carleton Coffin, of Boston; Mr. Linsley,
assistant engineer of the road; Thomas C.
Hawley, now of Lake Park; Mrs. Rice, Mrs.
Coffin, Mrs. Governeur Morris, of New York,
and two daughters, and Miss Audubon,
grand-daughter of the great ornithologist,
after whom the town of Audubon is named,
and J. Young Scammon, of Chicago. On
Monday the party went into Dakota some
twenty miles, and then striking south came
across to Fort Abercrombie and thence
back to St. Paul via Pomme de Terre,
Alexandria, Sauk Centre and St. Cloud.
Mr. Canfield left the party at McCauleyville,
and came back across the country on horseback alone, with some provisions in his
pocket, to examine more fully the proper
places for towns and to look out a line from
the Buffalo river for the railroad to the
height of land at Lake Park.

<h2 style="text-align:center">LOCATION OF BISMARCK.</h2>

In May, 1872, before the railroad track
had reached the Red river, while there was
but one white inhabitant west of it, he
crossed the plains with his horse and buggy,
accompanied by General Thomas L. Rosser,
Mr. Biy and others, carrying their own provisions from Moorhead, 200 miles to the
Missouri, while it was yet Indian Territory,
and located Fargo and laid out and located
Valley City, Jamestown and Bismarck, and
determined the point for the crossing of the
Missouri by the railroad, where the long iron
bridge now is. Great care had to be taken
in the selection of sites for the various towns,
so as to accommodate the surrounding country
after it should be settled up, but especial
care was important that the title to the land
should be perfect. Innumerable were the
difficulties that appeared in this respect—all
sorts of questions arose suddenly, various
and unexpected claimants turned up, which
required much patience and a knowledge of
the land laws to overcome. Great difficulties
were experienced with those towns west of
the Red river, because the lands were
unsurveyed, and especially because the panic
of 1873 came on before the railroad was
built in Dakota, which caused a suspension
of the work for two years, during which
time the various points had to be kept pos-
session of, at an enormous expense, by agents
residing there the year around in log huts,
the provisions for whose maintenance the
whole year had to be transported across the
country in summer, as no one would ven-
ture to make such a journey in winter.
The original log house at Jamestown, which
Merritt Wiseman, agent of the company,

occupied as a post for two years is still standing, as well as some of those occupied by the employés of the company at Bismarck.

Notwithstanding all the various claims made by different parties, whether under the homestead, pre-emption or town-site laws, or whether upon the surveyed or unsurveyed lands, the whole was so thoroughly examined and cleared up that there has never been a flaw found in the title to any of the lands or lots in these various locations, where now are flourishing villages and cities, and the deed or contract of the Lake Superior & Puget Sound Company is regarded as safe as a Government patent.

In November, 1871, Mr. Canfield crossed the desert 500 miles from Ogden on the Union Pacific Railroad, when there were very few settlers in that country, to Snake river near Shoshone falls; thence to Boise City, Idaho, and to Baker City, eastern Oregon, via the Burnt creek crossing of the Snake river, near where the Oregon Short Line Railroad now crosses; thence across the Blue mountains to Umatilla, on the Columbia river, and thence by steamer to Portland, Oregon, meeting there Mr. Rice, the vice-president of the company, who had preceded him via San Francisco and an ocean steamer, and with whom he was a committee of the Board of Directors to arrange for commencing the construction of the road from Columbia river to Puget Sound.

The alkali dust of the plains, so light that it rises like a cloud and covers everything the first mile traveled, which fills the hair and clothes, penetrates the eyes, ears, nose, mouth and throat,constantly irritating them and producing soreness; the scarcity of water and provisions, and the rough trails and difficult crossings of streams; the rather familiar attention of wild animals, with their ravenous demands upon himself and his teamster, his only escort most of the way, made this trip across the country the hardest by far he ever experienced.

While on the coast, this time he explored Puget Sound for the second time, accompanied by Mr. Rice and some engineers, and also went up the Columbia river as far as the Cascade rapids.

EXPLORATION OF PUGET SOUND AND LOCATION OF TACOMA.

While it always had been the intention and policy of the Northern Pacific Railroad Company to use the navigable waters of the lakes and rivers across the continent in the first instance and connecting the portages by railroad, in order to get a communication through the whole route as soon as possible, which would at first make the Columbia river route available and Portland the terminus of the branch line, and the commercial center of Oregon, yet Mr. Canfield always insisted that sooner or later the interest of the railroad would demand the construction of the short line across the Cascade mountains to Puget Sound. However much the views of the directors of that day may have been modified in favor of Portland as a final terminus in consequence of the obstacles presented by the Cascade range, he never subscribed to their views, but took the ground that the future great commercial city on the Pacific coast would be on the waters of Puget Sound, where it could be approached with ease through the Straits of Fuca by the largest vessels from all parts of the world, without being subjected to delays, damage and shipwreck by the bars which necessarily are formed at the mouths of the great rivers. Accordingly, he secured large tracts of land at various points on the sound from Olympia to Bellingham bay, and had a thorough examination made of all the bays and harbors, as well as of the country contiguous, as to the practicability of approach by a railroad, and the supply of fresh water for a city with reference to selecting a site for the future terminus of the Northern Pacific Railroad.

At Tacoma he purchased a large tract, believing it would be the point on the sound where a railroad from the south would first touch it, and connect it with the Willamette valley and all the immense productive country west of the Cascade mountains for hundreds of miles to California and beyond by branches to Utah and Nevada, at the same time being located, as it were, in front of the Cowlitz, Natchez, Stampede and Snoqualmie passes of the Cascade range, one of which he believed the railroad would, sooner or later, adopt as its crossing, as it would be the easiest point of access for the main line from the east, forming a junction at Tacoma with the lines from Oregon, California, Utah and Nevada from the south, even if in the future it should be deemed expedient by the company to continue the line down the sound to some point nearer to the entrance of the Straits of Fuca as the final terminus. The wisdom of this selection has since been demonstrated by the construction of a railroad from California to Tacoma, and by the extension of the main line from Lake Superior across the Cascade mountains through the Stampede pass to the same place, which although at the time of his purchase was a wilderness, is now a city of 20,000 people, at whose wharf float vessels from all parts of the world, exchanging the products of China, Japan and the Central and South American States for those of Washington and Montana, Dakota and the Eastern States.

Thus, through the agency of Mr. Canfield, the Northern Pacific Railroad Company has been enabled to secure a large tract of land on the Mediterranean of the Pacific, giving it ample facilities for its terminus, shops, buildings, side tracks, wharves and warehouses, approachable without difficulty by the largest vessels in the world, as well as enabling it to lay out a city upon a plan and scale which shall adequately provide for all the wants and comforts of future generations, and which shall be a fitting counterpart to one to be built at its eastern terminus on Lake Superior, at the mouth of the waters of the St. Louis river, where Duluth and Superior now are, and which shall be the great center of business of that empire of the Northwest now being so rapidly developed, and second only to Chicago in population and commercial importance on the great chain of lakes.

In the words of the late first engineer of the company, Mr. Johnson, "It should be the ambition of all who are instrumental in its growth to render it the queen city of the Pacific coast, the model city of the world. No unfriendly elements should be allowed to mingle in or mar its fair proportions. It should be in all respects a fitting exponent of the benign and elevating influence of our free institutions, and should occupy the very foremost place among the great cities of Christendom, reflecting upon the isles of the Pacific and the shores of Asia, over which it is destined to exert a vast influence, the light of the most improved civilization."

At this time, also, Mr. Canfield located Tenino, Newaukem, Skookum Chuck, Olequa and Kalama on the line between Tacoma and Portland. Kalama was selected because it was at the head of highwater navigation of the Columbia river, at the same time being near Coffin Rock, which was one of the few places where the Columbia river could be bridged. Kalama was the place on the Pacific coast where the Northern Pacific Railroad laid its first rail, and which was its headquarters for several years on that coast.

PURCHASE OF THE OREGON STEAM NAVIGATION COMPANY.

It was while here Mr. Canfield foresaw the importance which the Oregon Steam Navigation Company might be to the Northern Pacific Railroad Company, especially during the progress of construction and until the company should build their Portland branch. This was a company owning twenty steamers, navigating from the ocean at Astoria, the waters of the Columbia, Willamette and Snake rivers and Pend d'Oreille lake for thousands of miles into Oregon, Washington, Idaho and Montana Territories. It was principally owned by Messrs. Ainsworth, Thompson and Reed, of Portland, and Alvinza Hayward, of San Francisco, and had been built up from one small boat, each run by Capts. Ainsworth and Thompson, and one of the best and most systematically managed companies in this country. Upon their showing to Mr. Canfield a full statement of their business from the beginning, he commenced negotiations with them for the whole property, which finally resulted in Messrs. Ainsworth and Thompson meeting Mr. Canfield and Mr. Jay Cooke at the latter's residence, Ogontz, near Philadelphia, in the following winter, and the sale was consummated, the Northern Pacific Railroad Company buying three-quarters of the stock of the Oregon Navigation Company, and the original parties retaining one-quarter and agreeing to manage the property the same as they had done so long as the Northern Pacific Railroad desired. But unfortunately the control of the Oregon Navigation Company was lost in the panic of 1873. Subsequent events connected with the Oregon and Transcontinental Company have shown how important to the Northern Pacific was the Oregon Navigation Company, justifying the views originally entertained by Mr. Canfield of the importance of the Northern Pacific Company owning and controlling it.

In 1872 Mr. Canfield escorted a majority of the board of directors of the Northern Pacific Railroad to Oregon and Washington Territory, going via the Union Pacific Rail-

road in a special car to Sacramento, thence overland by stage and rail to Portland and Puget Sound. Messrs. Cass, Ogden, Wright, Billings, Stinson, Ainsworth and Windom, directors; Samuel Wilkeson, secretary of the company;Milnor Roberts,engineer;Dr.Thayer and Colonel W.S. King,of Minnesota, composing the party. This was the first time these gentlemen had visited the Pacific coast, and, as what they then saw would probably determine many important matters about the future of the company's affairs, especially the crossing of the Cascade range and the terminus, Mr. Canfield chartered a steamer and visited by daylight all the principal places on the sound from Olympia to Victoria and Bellingham bay, returning through Deception pass, being the first steamer that ever went through this pass back, of Whidby island, into Holmes' harbor, the best harbor on the sound, thence to Seattle, then a place of 3,000 people, on Elliott bay; then to Commencement bay, which was then surrounded by a wilderness, but it was subsequently settled upon as the terminus —being where Tacoma is now located. At that early day, with nearly 2,000 miles between Puget Sound and Lake Superior to be traversed by an iron rail, much of which was then unsurveyed or even explored, except by Mr. Canfield's expedition in 1869, the idea of crossing so high a range of mountains as the Cascades was not regarded by the directors as an easy matter, especially by those accustomed to building roads across the prairies; but Mr. Canfield took the ground that an enterprise of this magnitude would sooner or later demand the crossing of the mountains, and, although some who were present might not live to see that day, yet he predicted the demands of trade and commerce would be so great, that before 1890 trains would run from St. Paul and Duluth to the waters of Puget Sound without breaking bulk across the Cascade mountains, which prediction has been fulfilled three years in advance of the time named by him.

PREDICTION THAT LOUISBURG WILL ULTIMATELY BE THE EASTERN TERMINUS OF THE NORTHERN RAILWAY SYSTEM.

Twenty-three years ago Mr. Canfield visited the Island of Cape Breton, the last of December, and made an examination of Louisburg harbor, the best harbor on the Atlantic coast from Cape North to Cape Sable, with reference to the facilities for a shipping port, and he came to the conclusion then and still firmly believes, it will become the terminus of the northern chain of railroads across the continent, being only four days from Liverpool, with abundance of coal within ten miles. That the tea of China and Japan, and the spices of the Indies destined for Europe will go on board the cars at Tacoma, and not be transferred until put on board of steamers for Liverpool at Louisburg. It was one of the three-walled towns built on this continent although now entirely deserted, having been destroyed in 1760 during the French and English wars. It was once a city of 10,000 people and it was there that General Wolfe fitted out his expedition against Quebec. In fact, since Mr. Canfield was there the railroads have been extended from Montreal to within 100 miles of Louisburg, and a car of freight can now be shipped from Tacoma to the Straits of Canso, in Cape Breton, without breaking bulk, and it can not be long before this last 100 miles will be constructed. Then, with a train of Pullman Palace Sleeping and Dining cars standing on the wharf at Louisburg upon the arrival of a steamer from Europe with a load of sea-sick passengers on board, it will require no great stretch of imagination to determine how many will remain on board to make the rough passage along the coast when they can step on board the vestibule train, retire and be in Boston the next day to dinner and New York to supper.

The result of Mr. Canfield's experience is, he has traveled over nearly all the country between Lake Superior and the Pacific ocean via the northern route, on foot, or horseback, or muleback, in carts or wagons, long before the iron horse was heard in the land, and consequently has become familiar with the general topography and character of the country, and entertains the most sanguine views as to its great capacity in the future.

Few men comprehended so fully at an early day, even when St. Paul and Minneapolis were in their infancy, the great capability of this immense country—the fertility and extent of the Red River Valley, equal to that of the Nile—the abundant resources of various kinds awaiting future development between Lake Superior and Puget Sound—their capacity for easy and rapid development, such as no other country has ever before shown, which, combined with the facilities offered by the Northern Pacific and Manitoba, and other railroads yet to be built, to hasten settlements and accommodate the people, will create a great Northwestern empire, which will not only add incalculable wealth to the nation, but will form an important factor in its future government.

NEVER GAVE UP THE SHIP.

Amid all the ups and downs of the times —amid all panics and financial storms— notwithstanding all the discouragements of the early days of the Northern Pacific and the hostility of Congress to its applications— Mr. Canfield has always maintained the same abiding faith in this magnificent undertaking and the same confidence in its ultimate success, and he still believes it will become the great transcontinental highway across the continent to Europe, not only for the products of the farm, forest and mines along its border, but for the products of Japan

China and the Indies. In fact it will become the *World's Highway*, over which will pass the travel and business of the most enlightened and civilized portions of the globe.

In view of the great diversity of productions of this country, and those of the Central American States and the British Dominion, the commercial relations between them and the United States must be constantly growing stronger and stronger, until their interest shall be separated by no transatlantic influence or power. Having great faith in the wisdom and sober second thought of the people expressed through a free, unobstructed and universal suffrage, he believes that within a half century there will be but one English-speaking nation in North America, under a republican form of government, extending from the Atlantic to the Pacific, and from the Gulf of Mexico to the Arctic Ocean. A nation over which will float only one flag, that of the stars and stripes of the United States. One Republic, whose free and enlightened institutions will confer upon millions of people all the benefits of the highest and most enlightened civilization, and be the controlling power among the nations of the earth.

Mr. Canfield continued as president of the Lake Superior & Puget Sound Company and a director of the Northern Pacific Railroad until the bankruptcy of the company in 1873, when, upon its reorganization, it became the principal owner of the Lake Superior & Puget Sound Company, and no necessity existed longer for an active manager. Mr. Canfield resigned after having devoted over twenty years of the prime of his life to inaugurate and put into operation this magnificent enterprise, with which his name must be forever identified as its most active organizer and promoter in its dark days, when very few had the faintest idea it would ever amount to anything.

It is a little remarkable that during all these many years, amid all the various modes of transportation, and the millions of miles he has traveled and in so many different places where there were no roads or other conveniences, he has never met with any accident nor has he ever carried any firearms of any description for a single rod; has never had any serious trouble with the Indians or "roughs" of the frontier, although meeting them at times under not very agreeable circumstances, where, but for his quick perception, good judgment of human nature and discreet action, serious results might have occurred.

The board of directors of the Northern Pacific Railroad decided at an early day as soon as construction commenced not to become personally interested in any lands or property on the line of the proposed route; but the difficulty of getting emigrants to go into an unknown country with all their worldly effects, uncertain as to what the land would produce, compelled the directors to modify their policy to a certain extent, and to adopt one which Mr. Canfield had frequently laid before them, namely, that in order to demonstrate to the world the great fertility of the soil and its adaptability to farming, they should at distances of, say thirty miles apart, take up a section of land along the line in advance of settlements, break it up and sow it to wheat, and thus show by facts, instead of talk and advertisements on paper, what actually could be done. As he was the advocate of this policy, of course, it fell upon him to lead off, and he accordingly purchased about 5,500 acres in the Park Region of Minnesota, at Lake Park, at the point where the outer rim of the Red River basin connects with the timber region. Other directors, Mr. Tower took 3,000 acres at Glyndon, and Messrs. Cheney and Cass 6,000 acres at Casselton, Dakota, which has since become celebrated as the Dalrymple farm, being managed by Oliver Dalrymple, one of the oldest wheat raisers in the Northwest. All these were at once put under cultivation, and the enormous crops of No. 1 hard wheat the first year gave an impetus to emigration and settlement; thus the great farms which have been so much abused did more to advertise and develop the country and bring in emigrants and settle it up than $100,000 expended in advertising. Nowhere in the history of the world has such a rapid and extensive development been made as in northwestern Minnesota and Dakota, over 40,000,000 bushels of wheat having been raised this last year, besides all other crops, and that, too, mostly upon what was Indian territory in 1870, and where there was then no white inhabitant.

BACK TO FARMING WHERE HE BEGAN FIFTY YEARS AGO.

Mr. Canfield, since his retirement from the railroad company, has devoted more or less of his time to his farm at Lake Park, and has taken the ground that to make a farming country prosperous and successful it should not be confined to one single crop, like wheat, but all crops adapted to the soil and climate should be raised ; and he has endeavored to show what can be done by diversified farming. The beauties and advantages of the Lake Park Region, as well as the efforts of Mr. Canfield in demonstrating the advantages and importance of diversified farming, are strikingly described by an eminent writer and traveler, on his return across the continent a few years since, after having visited most parts of the United States. He says:

" That vast forest, the admiration of woodmen and the wonder of travelers, bordering on Lake Superior, as it proceeds westward, stoutly contests the earth's surface with open space and limpid lake. Gradually, however, the forest weakens, until here, thirty miles from the Red river, at about the highest northern point of the Northern Pacific Railroad, between Miles City and Duluth, it loses its hold, for westward are the unbounded unwooded prairies, always to be artificially watered, with exceptional cases, while surrounding and eastward is perhaps the most placidly beautiful country the eye ever rested upon.

" This connecting link contains the last lakes—if Devil lake be excepted—of size, and the last woods or forests for many hundred miles, and as such is not inaptly termed the Park Region, although hereabouts the Lake Park Region, from the name of this town, and is consequently about the only and nearest resort for the Dakotian of the plain for change of scenery, recreation and pleasure. The Park Region, taking this town as the objective point, extends sixty miles south to Fergus Falls, thirty north, is in width nearly thirty miles, while its altitude goes over 1,300 feet. It is unlike Dakota or Montana, for it is neither flat nor mountainous, but undulating, as the ocean, interspersed with lakes, groves, and an open, magnificent agricultural country. Within twenty rods of the depot is Lake Flora, a half mile wide, embowered with forest trees, and a half mile farther on is Lake La Belle, over two miles long, and well known for its pure waters and beautiful surroundings. Still in the same direction are other lakes, interspersed with farms, and vying in their admirable features. In Minnesota, according to the statistics of the land office, are over 10,000 lakes, and within fifty miles of Lake Park are 200 of these ; Lake Cormorant, in a direct line south a few miles, is the most westerly lake of size in Minnesota, easily accessible, has a gravelly beach of 100 miles, surrounded by wooded hills on three sides, variegated with forest-covered islands, abounding in fish and game, and capable of steamboat navigation. It must become the great summer resort in the future, and divide the honors with Lake

Minnetonka, especially for the citizens of Dakota. This Lake Cormorant in particular, and this Lake Park region in general, are the hunter's and fisherman's paradise, for on these hills are found game of various kinds, and in these lakes the finest-fiber fish, only waiting the angler's skillful hook.

"Renowned, however, as the Lake Park Region is becoming, and must continue to become as a summer region, its forests and farming lands indicate far more. What of these? The forests are inviting indeed and resemble cultivated parks, so much so that Bayard Taylor, who described them years since, alleged they bore a striking likeness to English parks in their stateliness, the grassy grounds underneath being devoid of underbrush and stumps. Those near by seem to be only fifty years old, and have caused much study to the scientific as to how they came there. Four and five miles out, however, they seem older, not so cultivated, and larger. In these forests are found the white oak, basswood, maple, ironwood, cottonwood, ash, birch, poplar, box elder and some other varieties. Their utility is easily seen, for in the open prairie the fuel question is an absorbing one; but when it is further stated that these thick forests cut off the fierce winds—the bitter, biting curses of the smooth prairies—their further provident use is apprehended. Thus these forests are not alone a thing of beauty, but of utility and protection.

"Now then as to the country between lakes and woods—the farming lands. It is divided up, more than in any other place visited, into farms of 160 acres. On each of these, almost without exception, are small lakes, so that with the natural grass, which is similar to the bunch grass of Montana—only the bunches are smaller and more frequent—they seem specially designed for the raising of cattle, horses and sheep. This grass, together with the pure water and atmosphere, makes the very best of milk, butter and cheese. The soil is a rich, black loam, from eighteen to thirty inches deep, with subsoil of clay, and has the same characteristics of the best portions of the Red River Valley, for the Lake Park Region is the eastern edge or rim. The Red River Valley wheat has attracted attention deservedly throughout the civilized world, and is the result of. the peculiar ingredients of the soil no less than the climate, and these together have produced the best Scotch Fife wheat in existence, known hereabouts as No. 1 hard, meaning Scotch Fife wheat, weighing, when cleaned, fifty-eight pounds to the bushel, often sixty and sixty-one pounds, and hard. Duluth and Minneapolis are its great markets. The latter with its vast mills turns out 20,000 barrels per day. This is done by means of a series of rollers. The first set cracks the kernels of wheat in two, then it passes through a bolt and purifier, then through a second set of rollers, cracking it finer than before; then more dross eliminated by bolt and purifier, and so on clean down to the last roller, bolt and purifier, and the final result is the most perfect flour in the world, so much so that it is shipped direct from there to Germany, England, Scotland, France, and is consumed in preference to any other by the best families in the United States. Now it will be perceived why the famous St. Louis flour and celebrated Richmond (Va.) flour has been literally superseded. The Red River Valley flour, bluntly stated, is for sale in the markets of the world. This is not all. The Red River Valley wheat, of which this region is part and parcel, is sought after by all the important milling centers in the United States. Why? To mix with inferior grades—tone them up so as to produce their 'superfine' flour. Thus in large quantities this famous wheat is in St. Louis, Richmond, Cincinnati, Rochester, Buffalo,

Boston, etc. The logical inference to be drawn from this is that the lands from which such wheat flour is produced must be not simply wonderful, but exceedingly valuable. They are valuable, however, in the additional fact that the Lake Park Region is the one naturally adapted to diversified farming. In order to understand this and some other points, a little digression will be necessary.

"Lake Park was located and laid out on the 4th of July, 1873, by the Lake Superior & Puget Land Company, which was organized as an auxiliary to the Northern Pacific Railroad Company, with the object of purchasing land at proper places for stations on the railroad, establishing ferries across rivers, and doing anything else which was necessary to advance the construction of the road and which the Northern Pacific Railroad Company could not do by their charter.

"Mr. Thomas H. Canfield, of Burlington, Vermont, was president of the former and director of the latter. Between these two positions his duties called him to critically examine sites, soils, climates, ingress and egress, depressions and elevations—in fact, nearly everything connected with the advancement and permanency of the Northern Pacific Railroad, and thus he located and laid out most of the towns from Lake Superior to the Missouri river, and many on the Puget Sound and Columbia divisions, and this is how he came to select and lay out Lake Park, in his opinion, as well as that of many others, the most desirable place on the whole line of road for beauty of landscape and variety of resources. It was difficult in the early days to get settlers on the railroad line. They were afraid of Indians, knew nothing about the soil, crops or climate, excepting vague rumors born of ignorance and incredulity. How then was this to be done? Why, 'if the mountain won't come to Mahomet, Mahomet must go to the

mountain;' in other words, the directors had to do it themselves, and this common-sense solution proposed by Mr. Canfield was carried out. It was absolutely necessary, for even after the railroad reached the Red river the settler would not go beyond, and, furthermore, at this time there was no settlement west of the Mississippi river north of the forty-fifth parallel, for this whole stretch of country was then considered by outsiders as Indian territory. In this solution of the problem, soils, crops, etc., as above stated, Messrs. Cass & Cheney selected about 3,000 acres each west of the Red river, near Casselton, Dakota, Mr. Tower nearly the same amount at Glyndon, Minnesota, and Mr. Canfield the farm he now occupies of 3,000 acres south of Lake Park, and 2,500 acres in the adjacent town of Cuba, three miles north, for Rev. Dr. Hawley, now of Brainerd, Minnesota, formerly of Connecticut, by whose happy suggestion this town received the appropriate name of Lake Park. On these two farms Mr. Canfield has most successfully carried out his ideas of diversified farming. The writer, in company with this gentleman, had the pleasure of examining these properties. His farm was seen first. It touches the railroad limits and extends south in one compact body. At about its center, on an eminence, was the large, elegant two-story residence of the foreman, surrounded by houses for workmen, fine barns for horses, sheds for cattle, a granary, and a warehouse 120 feet long by 30 feet wide for machinery, for this last is the feature of Western farming. The hands were threshing the wheat with the steam thresher at the rate of a thousand bushels per day, and there in the open field the bundles of wheat brought upon wagons were put into the machine and came out shelled and were immediately placed in bags and started for the railroad elevator, to be shipped to Duluth by the Northern Pacific Railroad. See by this the startling difference between the time of Abraham and the nineteenth century. Here were also some of the finest cattle, unexcelled by any seen in Montana, with such shapely limbs, elegant coats, silky, shiny hair, intelligent eyes—but who can describe them? The writer can not. They are beyond him, and are fit subjects for the wondrous tongue of Daniel Webster or the vivid brush of Rosa Bonheur. And now, what shall be said of the horses? They were the best and largest lot of blooded stock seen in this Western tour, for there was not a stick among them all. No wonder that a man likes to steal horses. The writer in looking at this magnificent lot felt like taking one himself. On the eastern part of this farm there is an unusual eminence, to which Mr. Canfield took the writer, which eminence could only be compared to the place where the devil took the Savior, not so much on account of its elevation as the vast stretch of vision it afforded. It was a clear, sunshiny day and the whole country was spread out before us. There were the groves, the lakes, the cattle, the horses, the fields of grain cut and uncut, the threshers in various directions, trains of cars on the Northern Pacific, and last, not least, over 300 farm houses, where ten years ago was not one. Never has the writer had such an extensive and varied view in every direction, not even from the highest elevation of the Rocky mountains. Mr. Canfield commenced operations on these two farms in 1876, and has now under the plow about 900 acres on one, and 600 on the other. He has built about fifty miles of fence composed of oak rails and barbed wire, introduced some of the best Short-horn herds of the country, superior blooded stock, until he now has 400 head of thoroughbreds and high grades. These have been bred with reference to form, best adapted to carry the greatest amount of muscle and fat, disposed in the

best manner to secure the choicest beef, at the same time having in view the strain possessing the highest qualities for milk and butter, thus making them particularly valuable for this section of the country, both for beef and the dairy. All these animals have been bred with care by the most experienced breeders, their pedigrees showing a line direct from some of the highest and best English stock. He has also purchased two Percheron Norman stallions from France, from which he has raised many superior colts as well as enabling his neighbors to do the same. This breed of horses is particularly adapted to a farm where so much machinery is needed. They weigh from 1,400 to 1,600 pounds each, and being fast walkers accomplish much more every day with the machinery than ordinary horses, and thus being strong in proportion they are a great profit in the course of a year by the excess of their strength and quickness. To those who have considered farming on a large scale, where the raising of grain is the main object, the unsolved problem has been how to keep their men and teams employed between seeding and harvest, and also in the winter season. This gentleman does this by cutting the natural meadow grass for the winter season, and letting his cattle run out on the pastures to fatten from spring to fall, and in the winter season both men and teams are at liberty to attend to them. Thus with scarcely any extra cost cattle-raising with its profits goes side by side with wheat-raising with its profits without in any way interfering."

" He has also made several valuable experiments, among which may be mentioned seeding with tame grasses, such as timothy, clover, red top, at sundry times, all of which have turned out well. He has, besides, adopted what is known in the East as 'summer fallowing,' and this also has been successful, for it gives the land a year's rest.

All these things and many others have been accomplished in six short years, and they reflect not only the untiring energy and consummate ability of this gentleman, but have forever settled the adaptability of the soil of Lake Park for wheat-raising, and what is more important, its peculiar natural adaptability for diversified farming, which system has since been adopted more or less by neighboring farmers. Much has been said in these latter days about 'large farms,' but the investigation of this and other sections demonstrates that they aroused the whole country and hastened the settlement of the Northwest by a decade of years; and nowhere along the Northern Pacific line is this more plainly visible than in the Lake Park Region. 'Never forget the bridge which carries you over.'

"The village of Lake Park is situated north of the Northern Pacific Railroad track, on a sloping elevation, admirable for sanitary and drainage purposes, overlooks the surrounding country, and has thus avoided those unfortunate divisions caused by being located both sides of the track or a half a mile apart. Thus the first impression—and it is everything to a stranger—is favorable. The second is the natural beauty of the town. Outside of its picturesque location, the lakes, the trees, the green grass, are beautiful as well as useful, and here they abound. The third and last impression indicated in innumerable ways is the iron tenacity and rigid economy of its citizens.

"The first settlers came to what is now called Lake Park in 1869, a few more in '70, not many additions in '71, but in 1872 houses commenced to be built. There were then twenty-five people, and the place had three names, viz.: Liberty for the town, Loring for the postoffice, and Lake Side for the railroad station. About 1876 the three, at the suggestion of the Rev. Dr. Hawley, were merged into Lake Park. The railroad reached here in 1871, and the cars have run regularly ever since. The greater portion of the people were Norwegians and Swedes, the rest Americans. All had come to this section to better their fortunes by cultivating the soil, although almost nothing was known about it. There is a tendency in the human mind to paint the rose without its thorn—the ocean without its tempests and hurricanes—the skies without their thunders and lightnings—the West without its clouds—as the material heaven. It looks in the apt words of the poet as if—

> 'Life is a sea;
> How fair its face;
> How smooth its dimpling waters pace;
> Its canopy how pure.'

"The reality, however, shows that—

> '——rocks below
> And tempests sleep
> Insidious o'er the glassy deep,
> Nor leave one hour secure.'

"The further history of this place proves the truth of the lines. During '70 and '71 very little wheat was sown, but that was consumed by grasshoppers. In '72 more wheat was sown, and that, too, was devoured by the grasshoppers. In '73 wheat was again sown—the grasshoppers didn't come, probably surfeited by their three years' feast; but what was not much better, cold and wet, and the crop was little or nothing. In '74 wheat was again sown, and grasshoppers ate up everything, probably hungry and mad because they gave the settlers a rest the year before. In 1875 another crop was put in. The weather was cold, but the grasshoppers wouldn't stay away. They knew too well the deliciousness of Red River Valley wheat, much better than some Eastern wiseacres, and desired once more 'to roll it as a sweet morsel' into their maws. The weather, however, killed them off, but not until they had destroyed some sections. The crop that year averaged twenty-five bushels per acre, which went sixty and clean up to sixty-four pounds to the bushel. Since then the grasshoppers have ceased their visitations, and the crop of wheat has been good, particularly during the last two years, including this present one. Many an American, during these five years of wheat famine, left for 'other fields and pastures new,' but the Scandinavian raised his 'garden sass,' killed muskrats, bartered the skins to the storekeepers to settle his grocery bills, and lived through, and the most of them are in a prosperous condition to-day.

"Lake Park derives its importance not simply from its surroundings and resources, but from its being located on that grand transcontinental route, the Northern Pacific Railroad, which Mr. Thomas H. Canfield, before alluded to in this history, spent the best part of his days in its dark and gloomy days to inaugurate. Pardon, reader, but if this gentleman would cease his active life (for he is an intensely busy man) and write a history of that road from its inception to date, how it was received and voted upon by distinguished men in public life, who would now hang their heads were their votes reprinted, how scientific, learned and profound men—not a few regarded him as visionary—who with seer-like vision prophesied the glories of the Northwest, and urged, with all the earnestness of his nature, its immediate adoption; how the project, after going up and down, received a gigantic impulse forward from 'Old Thad,' and was further accelerated by the cool, hard sense of Gen. Grant; how on the eve of success it fell through under the unfortunate, but to-day even misunderstood, financial operations of Jay Cooke, the ludicrous and humorous incidents connected therewith, as well as the serious; how it finally revived under President Villard, and has now been consummated, it would have all the intense interest of the best written novel, as well as the weight of authenti-

cated history. Yes, yes. The Northern Pacific Railroad is part and parcel of the history of Lake Park as well as the lakes, and this episode properly belongs here.

"On this road, 240 miles from St. Paul and 218 from Duluth on the one side and 1,700 from Puget Sound on the other, Lake Park is situated. Three passenger trains eastward and westward halt here each day as they pursue their journeys. Innumerable freight trains also go backward and forward, which not only interchange the products of States and Territories as now, but the best of Eastern and Western civilization; for the prophecy of Thomas Benton, 'There is India,' is no myth. Thus the reader will see that Lake Park is in the center of civilization and one of the most easily accessible places in the West.

"Thus Mr. Canfield has demonstrated that here is a section which can produce wheat equally as well as any other part of the Red River Valley, and in addition has the natural advantages for stock-raising. Although higher than Quebec, reaching near to the 47th parallel, this region in its quickness of growth, variety of crops, salubrity of climate and health of its people, is unsurpassed. To sum it all up: That he who would follow farming as an avocation, and not as a speculation, must do so on the diversified plan."

PERSONAL CHARACTERISTICS.

Mr. Canfield has now been engaged in active business forty-nine years, during which time he has never taken a day specially for recreation or pleasure, so called, but has found his pleasure in the work in which he has been engaged, believing thereby he was doing some good to his fellow-men and his country.

Although of a slender frame and fragile constitution, he is yet apparently as well and active and moves with the same elastic step as twenty years ago, which he attributes in a great degree to his constant busy life and temperate habits in all things, except work.

He is a good judge of human nature, enabling him to be an excellent organizer and manager of men, quick in observation, clear in judgment and rapid in execution. While being naturally self-reliant, to which his varied experience has contributed, yet he is ready at all times to listen to others and adopt their views, even if they differ from his own, if they have merit in them. Modest in his pretensions, he is ever ready to give to others the credit of any good work, although he may have been mainly instrumental in bringing it about. Having been engaged most of his life in work of a public character, and connected with many great enterprises, he has an extended knowledge of the country and broad and comprehensive ideas as to its capacity and resources, and entertains the most sanguine views as to its future greatness and power. When once enlisted in any scheme which commands his approbation, he is very persistent and perseyering until it is accomplished, no matter how difficult it may be or how serious the obstacles to be encountered. _The idea of defeat never enters into his calculations._ He is very retiring, talks but little, is a good listener, but clear in his ideas of right and wrong and firm in maintaining them. He is generous almost to a fault, and in anything in which he believes he is ready to back his acts with his money, so far as he is able; a true and firm friend to those who gain his confidence—and many are the men in good circumstances and prominent positions, in different parts of the country, who are indebted for them to his early aid and assistance.

He is averse to undue display and notoriety, disliking anything which smacks of "fuss and feathers," and dreads to appear before the public, unless his duties or the necessities of the work upon which he is engaged require it.

He is never so happy as when at his country home, on Lake Champlain, surrounded by his charming family, and joining in all the details of their plans and schemes with the greatest pleasure.

At different times he has been actively engaged in political matters, but always refusing to accept any office of any kind, preferring to aid those whom he deemed capable of filling public stations. Arriving at his majority when the old Whig party was prominent, his first vote was cast for its nominees, and he continued identified with it until it was succeeded by the Republican party, to which he has since belonged. He understands thoroughly all the great political issues which have agitated the country for the last forty years, as well as the great commercial questions which involve the business and prosperity of these United States. Few men have had a more extensive acquaintance and knowledge in the last generation of the prominent men of the nation, whether in politics or business.

A PROMINENT CHURCHMAN.

He is an active member of the Protestant Episcopal Church, having been brought up in it from childhood, the house in which he was born in Arlington, Vermont, being the one occupied by his grandfather, Nathan Canfield, the lay delegate to the first convention of the Diocese of Vermont, which was organized at Arlington in 1790; and, as will be seen from the above, his great-great-grandfather, Capt. Jehiel Hawley, had officiated as Lay-Reader of the Church service regularly on Sundays from 1764 until his death. He was baptized in infancy in the old original church at Arlington by "Priest Bronson," one of the first clergymen in Vermont, and confirmed by Bishop Hopkins in St. Paul's church, Burlington, Good Friday, 1848. He was for many years a vestryman and warden of St. Paul's church, had charge of the enlargement of the church in 1852, raising the money for it, and again in 1868 in building the transept, devoting much time as well as money. He has attended every convention of the Diocese of Vermont for thirty-seven years, twenty-eight of which he has been the secretary of it. For several years he was a member of the Standing Committee of the Diocese, and also represented it as Deputy in the five general conventions of the Church in the United States, held in Philadelphia in 1856, in Richmond, Virginia, in 1859, in New York in 1874, in Boston in 1877, and in Chicago in October, 1886.

Of the original incorporators and trustees of the Vermont Episcopal Institute, chartered in 1854, he and the Hon. E. J. Phelps, the present United States Minister at the Court of St. James, are the only survivors. He has been the resident trustee ever since, having charge of its affairs, and as treasurer for the last twenty-five years. He was closely identified with the late Bishop Hopkins in the negotiations for the 100 acres at Rock Point, Burlington, Vermont, for an Episcopal residence and church schools, and in the erection of the large stone building for the theological and academical departments. During the last two years he has been very active and instrumental in raising $60,000 for the buildings for the young ladies' department, and has had full charge of the erection of them upon the same property.

There is probably nothing which Mr. Canfield has done in his whole life in which he has taken more interest, or regards of more importance, than the erection of "Bishop Hopkins' Hall," at Burlington, Vermont, for the purpose of a church school for young ladies, not only on account of the high standard of intellectual, scientific and classical instruction maintained therein, but especially for the moral and religious culture which the pupils will receive through the elevating influences and Christian training of The Church. Considering the positions these young ladies may be called upon to occupy in different parts of our wide-spread land hereafter, whether as teachers, wives or mothers, their influence upon the civilization and improvement of the community where their lot may be cast must necessarily reflect the training and instruction received at their Alma Mater, and constitute a continual living force for all time to come, the usefulness of which to society, the church and future generations can not be estimated by any human mind.

Around a refined and well-ordered home, the center of which is the wife and mother, cluster the most intense affections and endearments of all—on them, under God, depend the most precious interests of the rising generation. The most persuasive and active influence in every religious work rests in their hands, and without them in these degenerate days we should have neither church, minister nor people, and how important then that their education have for its foundation the Christian religion.

Mr. Canfield regards the establishment of this institution as the climax of his life's work; and although perhaps of not as much magnitude in the estimation of the public as some other things which he has done, yet the real intrinsic good which it will confer upon mankind will be constant and perpetual; a high and important destiny awaits it — it will be a fitting exponent of the refined and elevated influence of our Church institutions, maintaining that thoroughness of intellectual, scientific and Christian education, whose solidity of structure and completeness of proportions will cause it to harmonize with all the beauty and grandeur of the teachings of The Church, as does the building itself with the beauty and grandeur of the magnificent and diversified scenery by which it is surrounded. He has

so managed the finances of this cor-
poration that the Diocese of Vermont has
now this beautiful property on the banks of
Lake Champlain, of 100 acres, with an Episcopal residence, a large stone building for
the theological department and boys' school,
and another of equal dimensions for the
young ladies' school, both in successful operation, and the whole paid for — *not a dollar
of debt outstanding or any lien upon the
property.*

He was mainly instrumental in raising
the money for building Trinity chapel,
Winooski, Vermont, the plan being prepared
by his brother-in-law, the Rev. Dr. Hopkins,
as was also that of the Episcopal church at
Brainerd, Minnesota, which he founded,
furnishing the block on which it stands and
half the money for the building. He also
furnished the sites for the churches at Moorhead and Lake Park, Minnesota, Bismarck,
Dakota, and Kalama, Washington Territory,
and assisted in building the churches. However much he may be absorbed in business,
he always finds time to attend to The
Church and its interests.

Few men have ever had a more busy life,
which from present indications is likely to
continue in the same way to the end; and
he probably will, as he says he expects to do,
"die in the harness."

CONCLUSION.

As the writer pens the closing sentences of
the life history of this truly great man, a
newspaper, the *Manchester Journal,* one of
the leading journals of Vermont, falls into
his hands, containing an article which forms
a fitting conclusion for this biography, illus-
trating the standing of Mr. Canfield in his
native State, the respect in which he is held
and the prominence he has attained. The
Rev. Dr. Wickham referred to in the article,
one of the most able men in Vermont, succeeded the Rev. Dr. Coleman as principal of
Burr Seminary for thirty years. The Editor
who had evidently written an article on
the Northern Pacific Railroad, for the
Manchester Journal says : " Rev. Dr. Wickham sends us a note, saying that he
was very greatly interested in the article on
the Northern Pacific Railroad. Thomas H.
Canfield was a student at Burr Seminary
just before Dr. Wickham came here, fifty-one
years ago, but the doctor was well acquainted
with him before he left Arlington, and went
down there at his solicitation and gave a temperance lecture to an association formed
mainly by the efforts of Mr. Canfield, then
considerably less than twenty years of age.
Dr. Wickham was then greatly impressed
with his energy and formed high hopes for
the future of the young man, which have not
been disappointed. Dr. Wickham adds :
' If Burlington can boast of her Edmunds,
the leader of the United States Senate, and
of Phelps, the eminent jurist and distinguished representative at the Court of St.
James, she has not another citizen that
has honored her more than Thomas H.
Canfield.' "